Bug Out! Part 3
Motorhome Madness

Robert Boren

South Bay Press

Copyright © 2014 by Robert Boren.

All rights reserved. No part of this publication may be reproduced, distributed or transmitted in any form or by any means, including photocopying, recording, or other electronic or mechanical methods, without the prior written permission of the publisher, except in the case of brief quotations embodied in critical reviews and certain other noncommercial uses permitted by copyright law.

Author/Publishing South Bay Press

Publisher's Note: This is a work of fiction. Names, characters, places, and incidents are a product of the author's imagination. Locales and public names are sometimes used for atmospheric purposes. Any resemblance to actual people, living or dead, or to businesses, companies, events, institutions, or locales is completely coincidental.

Book Layout ©2017 BookDesignTemplates.com
Cover Design: SelfPubBookCovers.com/RLSather
Bug Out! Part 3– Motorhome Madness/ Robert Boren. – 4th ed.
ISBN 9781973388791

For Landon

Government is not reason; it is not eloquence; it is force! Like fire, it is a dangerous servant, and a fearful master.

—George Washington

Contents

Previously - in Bug Out Part 2 1

The Two Militias 3

Unlikely Partners..17

The Cavalry Arrives...31

On the Run 45

Guns in the Distance 59

Body Disposal 73

Ambush!..85

Double Agents..99

Terror from the North 113

Heat of Battle 127

Dead Soldiers 143

Previously - in Bug Out Part 2

Frank and Jane and their fellow travelers were still on the road, leaving northern Arizona for southern Utah. On the trip they got the news of nuclear attacks in the ports of New York City, Seattle, and Vladivostok. They made it to a friendly RV Park in Utah, and were able to take a breather and watch the devastation of continued worldwide nuclear attacks on TV. They didn't relax for long, as it became obvious that they would need to defend themselves or run farther away. The group started to rely on each other, and made it through arguments and in-fighting to become a force to be reckoned with. Then, at the end of Part 2, there was murder. Somebody killed the short wave radio operator, and damaged the radio. Who did this, and why?

{ 1 }

The Two Militias

Frank and Jerry stood in the coach, looking at each other.

"You think somebody screwed up the radio on purpose?" asked Frank.

Jerry looked at him, and then glanced over at the bedroom door, as it slid open and Jane walked out. Then he looked back at Frank.

"Oh, I know somebody did it on purpose. They removed two diodes."

"Uh Oh, what happened?" asked Jane as she walked over.

"Somebody disabled the radio on purpose," Frank said. "Is it fixable?"

"Already fixed," Jerry said. "I always carry around spare electronic parts in case something in the coach craps out. I didn't have the exact same parts, but close enough. It works now."

The three of them were silent for a few minutes.

"Who else knows?" asked Jane.

"You two and Jasmine," Jerry said. "Rosie was already asleep."

"Alright, so who could have done this?" Jane asked.

"Well, let's think it through," Frank said. "Who wasn't at the Happy Hour last night?"

"I'd say who wasn't at the Happy Hour after dark," Jerry said. "I don't believe somebody did this in broad daylight."

"Alright, agreed," Frank said. "Charlie left for a few minutes."

"Not long enough," Jerry said. "In some ways I'd like it to be him, but these diodes are buried in that radio. It was a fifteen minute job just to get down in there to reach them. Charlie was only gone for about five minutes, remember? I don't think it was him."

"Jeb was gone for quite a while, but I can't imagine that he would do such a thing," Frank said.

"You like him, but how well do you know him?" Jerry said. "He kinda seems like a survivalist militia type to me."

"Jackson and Earl," Jane said.

"Oh, yeah, forgot about them," Jerry said. "Could have been only one of them, too. Maybe the Williams Militia planted them."

"Everybody else that I can remember was at Happy Hour," Frank said. "Of course, it is possible that an outside party did this."

"Officer Simmons?" Jane asked. There was a tremor in her voice.

"Oh, crap," Frank said.

"You guys are forgetting something," Jerry said. "What outsider knew that Arthur was the ham radio operator? This was not a random attack. This was planned, and by somebody who knows about radios. Somebody wants to keep us from talking to people on the outside in a way they can't control."

"We could still talk on the phone," Jane said.

"Yeah, until they disable the cell tower nearby, or cut the land line." Jerry said. "That is much easier to shut down than a short wave radio."

"So what do we do now?" asked Jane.

"I think we should keep quiet and watch. Wait for the Sheriff to respond," Jerry said. "And don't tell anybody that I fixed the radio. I'm going to make like I don't know what's wrong with it."

"We need to keep an eye on Jackson, Earl, and Jeb. And perhaps Charlie too, although he couldn't have actually done the deed himself without help," Frank said.

"Alright, I'm going to go back to my rig before we draw any more attention. Good night." Jerry turned and opened the door. He crept quietly back to his rig.

Frank locked the door behind him. Then he sat down on the couch. Jane was leaning against the kitchen counter.

"Is it time to leave?" asked Jane.

"Maybe," Frank said. "I say we sleep on it."

"It's probably the Williams Militia," Jane said. "Jeb is a survivalist. Maybe he's a plant."

"I'm thinking about that, but there are some problems. He was a bloody mess earlier in the evening. No way could he have gone into Arthur's rig like that without leaving something behind."

"How about after he cleaned up?"

"Maybe, but then how much time would he have had?"

"There's a lot of tension between him and Charlie," Jane said.

"True, but its old friend tension. They care about each other. You can see it. We should watch him, though."

"Agreed. The thing that scares me the most is that it could be almost anybody. And I don't completely buy the story that this couldn't have happened in broad daylight. It could have happened between the start of Happy Hour and dusk quite easily. That opens up the field to a lot of people."

"True," Frank said.

"Where's that hand cannon of yours?"

"In my bedside table drawer."

"Good, make sure it's loaded. I don't feel safe."

"Yeah, neither do I," Frank said. "I'm glad we have Lucy with us. Nobody is getting close to us without our little four legged burglar alarm going off."

"That's true. She buys us enough time to wake up and take aim."

"Want to try to get to sleep?" Frank asked.

"Yes, I think we should. I think we should be up early tomorrow."

Frank got up and headed to the bedroom. He turned on the light and opened his bedside table drawer. The gun was there. He checked it. Fully loaded. He put it back in the drawer, and started changing into his PJs.

"It's ready to go?" asked Jane, as she came in the door and pulled off her robe.

"Yes, it's good. Safety is on, but you know how to take that off, correct?"

"Yes, but I don't know if I could hit anything with that monster."

"I'll tell you what. I'll go get the shotgun and lean it up against the wall by your side of the bed."

"Alright, that would make me feel better."

Frank went into the front of the coach, and came back in with the shotgun. He leaned it against the corner by Jane's side of the bed, and then slid the bedroom door shut. The two got into bed. Even though they were both keyed up, they were tired too, and they fell asleep within minutes.

Frank awakened with a start. He had busy dreams all night, and didn't feel very well rested when the sun came through the side window. Jane was already out of bed. He could hear her puttering around in the kitchen.

"Good morning," he said as he walked out of the bedroom. "Sleep okay?"

"Not bad, considering. You tossed and turned a lot."

"Sorry. Busy dreams. I'll throw on my shorts and take Lucy out."

"Good, thanks. Cereal alright this morning?"

"Sure, sounds fine." He went back into the bedroom and changed into his shorts. When he walked towards the door, Lucy was jumping up and down with her tail wagging.

"She's ready," Jane said, laughing.

"Yep," Frank said, as he picked up the leash and put it onto her collar. "Be back in a few minutes."

Bug Out! Part 3 – Motorhome Madness

Frank opened the door of the coach and stepped out, following Lucy down the steps. She did her usual....pulled Frank all over the campground. Frank looked around. It was a peaceful sunny morning. Nobody walking around yet, but the smell of coffee and bacon flowed with the gentle breeze. Morning was one of the times he loved best. He thought about his first cup of coffee and was anxious to get Lucy back into the coach. Nothing tasted as good as coffee on a camping trip.

Suddenly he heard the sound of a vehicle on gravel. It was the sheriff's car. It pulled up next to the office, and Sheriff Brown got out and went in the door. He was alone this time. Frank turned Lucy back towards the coach and guided her to the door.

"The Sheriff just arrived at the office," Frank said as he walked in. He unhooked Lucy's leash.

"Really, this early?"

"Well, it's already 8:30. I know it seems early to us retired types," he said, grinning. "I was at it for well over an hour by this time when I was working."

"True. Here's breakfast for our kids," she said, handing the bowls to Frank. He set them down, and the animals attacked.

"The Sheriff must think there's something to Jerry's story if they're back here this early," Frank said.

"Or maybe they made contact with some next of kin," Jane said. She stuck a coffee pod in the machine and put Frank's cup under it. The delicious smell filled the coach.

"Now that's what I'm talkin about," Frank said. When the brewing was finished Jane handed the cup to him. "Mmmmmmm, that's good."

"I'm on my second already," Jane replied. "Look, Hilda is walking the sheriff over to Arthur's rig."

Frank looked out the kitchen window. The sheriff was carrying a little black leather bag with him.

"Interesting. I'll bet that's a fingerprint kit."

"Won't your fingerprints and Jerry's be in the coach? And Cynthia's?"

"Yes, but we were all seen at Happy Hour until the time that the body was discovered."

"Shoot, you know who else wasn't there?"

"Who?"

"Cynthia," Jane said.

"You don't think she could have done it, do you?"

"Doubtful," Jane said. "But in reality, we don't know any of these people very well. What's it been, a little over a week since we got on the road?"

"Yeah, you have a point."

Frank got up and made himself a bowl of cereal. He brought it over to the dinette and sat quietly, eating and thinking. Jane watched him. She was leaning up against the kitchen counter, taking the last couple sips of her coffee.

"What should we do today?" Jane asked.

"Do you want to leave?"

"Yes and no," she said. "Do your worries about being on the road by ourselves still bother you?"

"Yes," Frank said. "Let's turn on the TV and see what's been going on. It's been a while since we caught up."

"Alright," Jane said, picking up the remote. "Local, CNN or Fox?"

"Either one of the nationals first," Frank said.

"OK." When the TV picture came up, Jane went to CNN, and sat down on the couch.

The pictures on the newscast were of New York City. Rubble that was much more widespread than the damage on 9/11.

"The lower half of Manhattan, along with Brooklyn, Jersey City, and the northern part of Staten Island are completely devastated," the announcer said. *"And radiation has been swirling around the entire*

Bug Out! Part 3 – Motorhome Madness

area, making the rest of Manhattan and the surrounding area dangerous. Evacuations to the north are ongoing. New York City will no longer be our greatest city. This is a sad time for the United States of America."

"This is so horrible," Jane said. "I always expected another terror attack eventually, but I didn't dream of something like this."

Frank sat quietly, trying to hold back tears.

"New York City was not the worst attack on the west," the announcer said. "Paris was hit with a larger device, in an area even more densely populated," the announcer said. "The City of Light has been darkened, perhaps permanently."

"The action must have slowed down," Frank said. "They haven't said anything about new attacks."

"I'll switch over to Fox," Jane said. She changed the channel. The picture on the screen was of Jerusalem.

"There is still sporadic fighting in the Middle East," the announcer said, "but the bombings have wiped out an enormous number of people. There are still remnants of the Caliphate active in the areas between the major population centers. They are saying this is just the beginning. Israel has been working with the Egyptians to take them out as they pop up. The humanitarian crisis here is unbelievable. Very little help is coming from the West, due to their own devastation. Israel and Egypt are trying to help, but even now the Islamic peoples are largely refusing any help if they know it is coming from the Jewish state. People wondered how WW III would look. This is it."

"Closer to home, the fighting is growing more intense in Mexico and Central America," the announcer continued. "There are still a large number of Islamist fighters in the area, and they appear to be getting re-supplied, although the source of that is unclear. They are setting themselves up in highly populated areas, using residents as human shields, which has slowed down the coalition of US and Mexican troops. To add to this mix, gangs of Mexican Nationalists, which appear to be working with remnants of the drug cartels, are trying to fight both sides and take Mexico back. This is helping the Islamists to survive."

"Geez, it's not going to be safe for a while, is it?" Jane asked. "Our military is going to be tied up there for years."

Frank nodded.

"Meanwhile the US is coming under harsh criticism by the UN because they have completely locked down the northern border of Mexico. ICE is no longer letting people come in and surrender. They are shooting anybody who refuses to turn around. The US Department of Homeland Security is telling the UN that they will not let potential terrorists into the United States. There have been some demonstrations against this in the US, but American citizens are attending those and shouting the protesters down in massive numbers. Violence breaks out often, and the protesters are starting to slow down on their activities. The police have been getting in-between the pro-immigrant protesters and citizens, but continue to stay on the sidelines when pro-Islamist demonstrations are attempted."

"Wow," Frank exclaimed. "Why don't people understand that we need to lock things down? Look around."

"Let's see if there is anything on the local channels," Jane said. She surfed through the channels until she found some local news.

"Three more groups of Islamic Terrorists were caught at the Canadian border yesterday, and are in custody in Everett, Washington at this hour," the announcer said. "Authorities warn that some groups have likely gotten through. Security around northern cities has been heightened, and Canada has begun to round up foreign nationals associated with the people who have been apprehended."

"Oh, no. Sarah," Jane gasped.

"So much for the north being safe. This is a huge problem, because we've never done much to secure the border with Canada. There are miles and miles of forest that they could just walk through up there."

"In other news, there has been some success in Arizona," the announcer said. "Phoenix is now back in the hands of the US Army, and the remnants of the Islamist army have fled to the northeast. Now that the battles for the major cities are over, the Army is putting all of its resources into the pursuit of the Islamists, who are trying to link up with the remaining fighters to the east of Flagstaff."

"Good," Frank said.

"There are two secessionist militias that are still causing problems in the western and northern parts of Arizona. State Police, local Sheriffs and other law enforcement have been trying to neutralize these groups while the Army is busy with the Islamists to the east. The larger of the two militias started in Yuma, and has been attempting to move northward along the Colorado River. The second militia, started in the Williams area, was forced to leave Williams and head north by the local authorities. They are now believed to be just south and east of the Grand Canyon. Authorities are keeping an eye on this situation carefully, because of the possibility that the southern militia is attempting to join the northern militia. If that were to happen, it would be a problem for the Army, as they would quickly overrun local authorities."

"Crap," Jane said. "We aren't even close to out of this mess, are we?"

"Doesn't sound like it to me."

"What should we do?"

"I think we continue to wait and watch at this point," Frank said. If the Army takes out the Islamists, maybe we should try to cross New Mexico and head into northern Texas."

"Or maybe we should just try to get back to California," Jane said.

"Yes, that's another idea. Maybe the best idea, if we can figure out a way."

"I wonder if we could go through Nevada and hit the middle of California from the east? Maybe up by Tahoe."

"There's some treacherous driving up there. Not sure I'm ready to drive this behemoth through Donner Pass."

"We could go up into Idaho, over to Oregon, and down from the north."

"Yeah, and maybe pick up Sarah on the way," Frank said.

"I'd like that," Jane said. "Look, the sheriff is coming out of Arthur's coach."

Frank looked out the window.

"Looks like he's coming this way," he said.

"And Hilda is making for Jerry's rig."

Lucy started to growl and bark as the Sheriff came to the door. Frank opened it.

"Good morning, Sheriff Brown," Frank said, as Jane tried to quiet Lucy down.

"Good morning, folks. Could you come down to the clubhouse with me, please? We have some things to discuss."

"Of course," Frank said. "Jane, why don't you turn on the AC so we can leave the critters in here?"

"Will do," she said.

They came out of the door of the coach, and Frank locked it up. Hilda was walking towards the office with Jerry and Jasmine. Hilda stopped at Cynthia's coach and asked her to join them.

They all arrived at the clubhouse at the same time. Hilda unlocked the door.

"Good morning, everybody," she said. "I'll get some coffee going."

"Have a seat," Sheriff Brown said. He motioned over to the first table. "Don't be nervous, folks. None of you are in trouble."

"The coffee will be ready in about ten minutes, for anybody that wants it," Hilda said as she walked over. She sat down with the group.

"Thanks for coming over," Sheriff Brown said. "As you probably guessed, we have questions about Arthur. His death was not of natural causes. As Jerry pointed out to me last night, he was smothered with a pillow. We were able to prove that at the coroner's lab."

"Horrible," Jane said. "I was hoping it wasn't going to be this kind of thing."

"Yes, we all were, Jane," said Hilda.

"Where's Charlie?" asked Jerry.

"He wasn't there last night until Hilda told him about it, so we didn't want to bring him in. Jerry, did you get a chance to look at the radio yet?"

"Yes, Sheriff Brown. I can tell you without a doubt that it was disabled on purpose."

"How can you be sure?" he asked.

"Somebody took the radio apart and removed two diodes. They knew exactly what they were doing."

The sheriff got a concerned look on his face.

"Alright, then we know that somebody killed Arthur to take away access to the radio. Is it fixable?"

"Already fixed," Jerry said. "I had parts in my tool box that worked."

"Good. Don't tell anybody outside of this room. Does anybody else know yet?"

"Just my mom," Jasmine said. "We told her this morning."

"She's back at your rig?"

"Yes. She's old and frail, and doesn't get around very well. I didn't see a reason to bring her."

"That's fine," the Sheriff said. "So I'll get to the point. We know that the Williams Militia is sending scouts up this way. We've caught two of them in the last 24 hours."

"No," Hilda said.

"It gets worse. Have any of you heard of the Yuma Militia?"

"Jane and I just watched a story on them before you came to our coach," Frank said. "They're working their way north along the

Colorado River, according to the reports. They said it would be bad if the Yuma Militia and the Williams Militia linked up."

"The Yuma Militia and the Williams Militia are one in the same," Sheriff Brown said. "They're split up right now, but are attempting to link back up. We are trying to trap them in the same place if possible. We want them to link up. The media is saying that the Army is completely tied up fighting Islamists in Eastern Arizona. That is only partially true. The militia is more dangerous than the remaining Islamists. The Army is close by, and they plan to set a trap."

"They aren't going to use us for bait, I hope," Jane said.

"No, that isn't their plan. But they don't want any of you to leave here just yet. They don't want to spook the militia."

"How much danger are we in?" asked Frank.

"I won't lie to you. There is some danger. For some reason the militia was interested enough in this group to put a mole among you. That's who we think killed Arthur."

"Any idea who that is?" Jerry asked.

"I'm hoping you folks can help us with that, Jerry."

The crack of a gunshot punctuated the air from the back of the park. First one, then another. Then two more.

"Everybody stay here!" Sheriff Brown yelled. He slipped out the door.

{ 2 }

Unlikely Partners

There were two more shots after Sheriff Brown ran out the door of the clubhouse. Jerry jumped off of his seat and ran to the window.

"Jerry, don't go by the window," shouted Jasmine. He got down and peered over the window sill. Frank started to get up. Jane shook her head no. Cynthia and Hilda were both sitting, looking at the open door, afraid to move a muscle.

After a few minutes, the Sheriff came trotting back in, breathing hard.

"Hilda, did you guys post somebody in one of Jer's old deer blinds?"

"We were going to start doing that. Even have a schedule in the works, but we didn't start it last night," she said.

"Jeb," Jane said. "Remember, he wanted to hang out up there and have a couple of drinks?"

The Sheriff gave her a quizzical look, and then got a smile on his face.

"Wait a minute, is Jer's stuff still up in that main blind?"

Frank laughed. Then Charlie came running in.

"What's going on?" he demanded. Then he saw the Sheriff and the rest of the group. "Hilda, are you having a meeting without me?" He had a hurt look on his face.

"No, sweetie," she said. "Sheriff Brown asked to talk to the people who were at Arthur's coach last night. You weren't there until after I told you about it."

Charlie nodded, but he still looked a little hurt, and a little suspicious.

Jasmine's phone started to ring, and she answered it. She listened, and then took the phone away from her ears.

"It's mom," she said. "Jeb is calling for help. She didn't think we would hear it up here."

"Let's go," Frank said. "I'm stopping by the coach to get my gun." Jane nodded, looking worried.

"I'm with you, Frank," Jerry said. They ran out the door, followed by the Sheriff.

"Slow down, guys!" Sheriff Brown yelled.

"Our friend is out there," Jerry yelled back. He ducked into his rig and came out with his M-1 Carbine.

Frank got to the coach, and Lucy was going nuts. He opened the door and she ran out, looking warily around. Frank grabbed the pistol, put it in the holster in a hurry, and belted up, and then grabbed his Winchester. He slipped the leash on Lucy and brought her too, then got out and met up with Jerry and the Sheriff.

"You brought the dog?" asked Jerry.

"My eyes and ears," Frank said, then he looked towards the blind and shouted. "Jeb, where are you?"

"Up in the blind, shot in the leg. I think I got all of them, but I'm not sure. Be careful. Bring a dog if you have one."

Frank laughed nervously.

"Oh, I've got a hell of a police dog," he shouted, and he bent down and took the leash off of Lucy, hooking it on the fence next to the gate. "Stay close, girl."

"Why did you take the leash off?" Jerry asked.

"The Winchester takes two hands," he replied.

The Sheriff crouched down. He had his service revolver in his hand.

"A little less chatter, you guys, there may be more of them out there."

Frank nodded.

"Should have grabbed the shotgun," Jerry whispered.

"You guys left too quick for that," he said.

"Watch out," Jeb yelled. Then there were several shots. One of them hit a tree next to Jerry. All three of the men hit the dirt. Lucy looked towards where the gunfire came from. It was like she was pointing. Frank saw where she was looking, and then got a bead on the spot with the Winchester. It was a bush next to a tree. He saw a slight movement.

"Got ya!" Frank said, and he pulled the trigger. A loud blast came from his Winchester. He saw a man fall. He worked the lever on the rifle to reload.

"Nice shooting," Jeb shouted.

"You can thank my dog. She pointed him out," Frank yelled.

"You're fighting modern weapons with that relic? Geez." the Sheriff said.

"Got the job done," Frank said. "Holds ten rounds, too."

"See any more?" shouted Jerry.

"No, but I'll keep my eyes open," Jeb said. "Come on forward."

The three men and Lucy walked slowly forward, scanning the landscape. They were almost to the blind when Lucy growled and looked again. The three men dropped to the ground. Frank and Jerry both looked at where Lucy was pointing.

"Got him," Jerry said, aiming the M-1 Carbine. He fired four times. The person got up and started running. "Damn .30 Carbine."

"I got him," Frank said, and then there was the blast of the .44 Mag Winchester. The running man flew about four feet and then hit the ground. Frank worked the lever to get another round into the chamber.

"What the hell are you shooting?" asked Jeb.

"Winchester Model 94 in .44 Mag," Frank shouted.

"I got to get me one of those," Jeb said.

They got to the tree that the blind was in.

"Can you climb down, Jeb?" asked the Sheriff.

"I'd rather stay up here. There's still booze left." He cracked up.

"Well, you guys are cool under fire, I'll give you that," the Sheriff said. "Seriously, do I need to get the fire department over here?"

"I got shot in the thigh, but got a tourniquet on. I haven't lost much blood. I can probably hobble down with my arms and my good leg. I didn't want to do it without somebody to cover for me, though."

"You have a rifle up there?" asked the Sheriff?"

"Yeah, my .270 Remington. I'm out of rounds, though. Didn't expect action this morning. I'll leave it up here, and maybe one of you guys can go up and get if for me after I'm down."

"OK, Jeb, why don't you start down," Frank said. "I'll keep watch with my police dog here."

"Hey, this is interesting," Jerry said, standing over by the bush where the first dead person was. "We have three dead Islamist fighters, and three guys that look like militia folks to me."

"What?" asked the Sheriff.

"Hey, get me down first, then you can investigate," Jeb said. He was already about halfway down the ladder.

"Don't worry, we're watching," Frank said. "Keep on coming."

"Finally," Jeb said as he put his good foot on the ground. "I'll need some crutches for a while, I suspect."

"You need a doctor," the Sheriff said. "I'll call for an ambulance.

"You might want to inform the Army that the militia and the Islamists are working together," Jerry said.

"Alright, let's go back to the park," the Sheriff said. "I'll radio for help."

"Somebody should hang out in the blind and keep watch," Jerry said.

"I'll do it," Frank said. "I've got a lot of ammo on my belt. And we know this sucker has some stopping power."

"True that," Jeb said. "How is that thing to shoot?"

"Kicks like a mule. It's shorter and lighter than the 30-30 model."

"I'll get up there and bring down your .270," Jerry said. He quickly climbed up the ladder and came down with it. "Maybe it will make a temporary crutch."

"Well, at least a cane," Jeb said, grabbing it from Jerry. "Dang, the barrel is still hot."

Frank climbed up the ladder and set his Winchester up there, as Lucy looked up at him and cried. Then he came back down, scooped her up, and carried her up to the blind.

"I'll keep an eye out until you get help here," Frank said. "Don't let Jane come out here after me."

"I'll try," Jerry laughed. "You know how these women are."

"That I do," Frank agreed. "Wonder if it's too early for a drink?"

The Sheriff shook his head as he was helping Jeb back to the gate. Jerry hurried to catch up to them.

As soon as they got into the gate, the Sheriff pulled out his cellphone and called Hilda.

"Hilda? Jack here."

"What happed back there?" she asked. She sounded scared.

"Tell everybody that our folks all survived," he said, "but Jeb got shot in the leg. Do you have any crutches or a walker or a wheel chair?"

"No walkers," Jeb said.

The Sheriff and Jerry chuckled.

"I heard that," Hilda said. "Tell that old reprobate that he'll take what I give him and like it."

"I don't think I want to tell him that, Hilda." He laughed.

"Alright, I do have a set of crutches, which were Jer's from when he broke his hip. I'll grab them and meet you guys."

"Thanks, Hilda," he said. He put the phone back in his pocket.

In the clubhouse, everybody was still afraid to move. Hilda looked at the women sitting at the table.

"What's going on?" Jane asked.

"Everybody is alive, but Jeb's hit in the leg. I need to get some crutches out to him." She went into her house, which was in back of the clubhouse, and took the crutches out of the hall closet. Then she went out with them to meet the men. She watched Jeb trying to use his rifle as a cane and shook her head.

"I hope that gun isn't loaded, the way you are using it," she said.

"Oh, it's empty alright. The bullets are stuck in some bad guys back there," he said with a grin. He took the crutches and got them under his arms, and then shifted to one side so he could get his rifle on his back with the sling.

They were just about to the veranda on the clubhouse. The Sheriff went off towards his car and got on the radio. He made several calls, and joined the others inside.

"Alright, the doctor's on his way. I also got the Army sending somebody, so we can discuss what happened back there."

"Good," Jerry said. He sat down next to Jasmine, and she slid close and hugged him.

"Where's Frank?" Jane asked.

"He is in the blind, keeping an eye out until the cavalry shows up," Jeb said.

"You left him out there alone?" Jane cried.

"No, he's not alone," Jerry said. "He's got Lucy with him, and that .44 mag lever gun. He'll be good for a few minutes."

"By the way, you've got one hell of a dog there," Jeb said. Jerry nodded in agreement.

"What do you mean?" Jane asked, still visibly upset.

"That damn dog saw the last two bad guys and pointed to them. We just had to look where she was looking."

"I'm not happy about him being there alone," she said.

"Ah, he's pretty safe up there," Jeb said. "The walls are thick enough to stop bullets."

Jane snorted. "You got hit."

"My own fault. I wasn't expecting company, so I had the door open. They got me with the first shot. Killed four of them after that."

"Who's them?" asked Hilda.

"Three Islamist fighters, and three militia men," Jerry said.

"What!" Jane said. "Jeez, nobody has any good info around here. Were they working together or fighting each other?"

"Working together, definitely," Jeb said. "The person who shot me was a militia guy. He's also the first one I shot. Traitor."

"So the Army has the situation all wrong?" asked Jasmine. "That's not very encouraging."

"You're telling me," Jane said.

A siren sound floated in from the distance, getting closer and closer. Then the fire department emergency vehicle pulled up in front of the clubhouse, and two paramedics piled out.

"Where's the doc?" the Sheriff asked.

"Right behind us," the first paramedic said.

They heard another car pull up, and the door open and close. The doctor came running into the clubhouse with his black bag.

"Where is he?" asked the doctor.

"I'm right here, Doc," Jeb said.

"Jeb, I didn't know it was you."

"Yep, it's me, George. Be gentle."

"You'll probably heal up on your own, you old bushwhacker," the doctor said as he approached. "Let's take a look. Lay down on that table."

Jeb hoisted himself up. The doctor came alongside him and put his black bag down on the bench next to the table. He opened it up and pulled out some scissors.

"No, you aren't going to cut my pants, are you? Can't I just take them off?"

The doctor looked at him and laughed, and then started cutting. After he got the pant leg out of the way, he untied the tourniquet. He got closer, and then pulled out a small LED flashlight and shined it on the wound.

"This is only a flesh wound…..the bullet went clean through. You're lucky, though. Another inch this way and it would have nicked the artery. I'd say you got shot by a military round. No expansion that I can see."

"Good," the Sheriff said.

"I'll let the paramedics clean this up and bandage it for you," the doctor said. He looked over at them. "Hey, guys, use plenty of iodine. Let's make it sting." He laughed, and the paramedics cracked up too.

"That's not nice, Doc," Jeb said.

"Any of the enemy need attention?" asked the doctor.

"You know, doc, that's a good question," the Sheriff said. "I assumed that they were all dead, but some of them may just be unconscious."

"The ones with half their brains hanging out are probably dead," Jerry observed drily. "Looked kind of like .270 to me."

"Damn straight, baby," Jeb said.

"You were using that old Remington bolt action of yours against these guys?" asked the doctor. "You're pretty brave."

"It's not how fast you shoot, it's how well you shoot," Jeb said. "Owwwwwww! Watch it with that stuff."

"Make sure you get plenty of that iodine in there, boys," the doctor said with a grin.

"Are there any who aren't obviously dead?" asked the doctor.

"Well, the one that Frank shot got it in the torso, but that was a .44 mag hunting round, copper on lead, so he's probably a mess inside. Big slow moving bullet. He only got hit once, though. The other one got hit at least twice with .30 Carbine but got up and ran, and Frank finished him off with a chest shot from the .44 mag. I doubt if either of them are alive, but it might be worth checking."

"Wait a minute, Frank killed two men?" Jane asked. She had a horrified look on her face.

"Lucy helped, don't forget," Jerry said. "And I helped on one of them. He doesn't get all the credit."

"You guys are sick," the Sheriff said. "Really."

The paramedics were done closing up Jeb's dressing. They looked over at the doctor. He nodded, and they gathered up their stuff and left.

"I thought Charlie would be down here. Where is he?" asked Jeb.

"He thought somebody ought to be watching the front of the park, so he's up on the roof of the store," said Hilda.

"Oh. Good idea," Jeb said. "He's a better shot than I am, and he's got better eyes too."

"So you guys have the front and back at least partly covered," the Sheriff said. "That's good."

"Should we be staying here?" asked Jane.

"If I were you folks, I'd probably stay here rather than get out on the road right now," the Sheriff said, "been hearing some bad things."

"I'm getting to where I don't trust anything you local folks say," Jane said. "No offense, but we've gotten *bad* info from people saying they had *good* info ever since we left LA."

"She's right," Jasmine said. "We need people to level with us about the situation around here. And we aren't going to be held here because the Army doesn't want us to spook bad guys. That's not how we operate in this country."

"Here here," said Cynthia. It was the first time she said anything since the shooting started. She didn't look good. She looked terrified and exhausted. The doctor walked over to her, and they had a hushed conversation.

"You are free to go if you feel you must," the Sheriff said, looking over at Jasmine. "But think carefully about it."

"We have a crowd of people heading this way," Jerry said as he looked out the window. "Took them a while to get out from under their beds after all the shooting, I guess."

Hilda looked over at Jerry with an annoyed expression. Then she walked out onto the veranda to greet them.

"What's going on?" asked Earl. Jackson was next to him, and the rest of the people gathered around.

The sheriff joined Hilda on the veranda before she could start talking.

"Hi, Folks," the Sheriff said in a loud voice. "I'm sure you heard the gun battle this morning. It appears to be over at this point."

"Who was it?" asked Earl.

"Three Islamist fighters and three militia men," he replied.

A murmur went through the crowd.

"Were they fighting each other?" asked Jackson.

"No, it appears that they were working together."

"Who shot them?" asked Earl.

"Jeb, Frank, and Jerry."

"It's important that we don't panic," Hilda said "We have Frank in the blind at the rear of the park keeping watch now, and Charlie is on the roof of the store watching the front of the park."

"Yes," the Sheriff said. "The Army's also on their way here."

More murmurs from the crowd.

"You mean an officer, or a bunch of troops?" asked Jackson.

"Probably an officer and a junior officer," the Sheriff said.

"You are welcome to hang out in the clubhouse if you'd like," Hilda said. "I made up some coffee earlier, and it ought to be ready now."

"Sheriff, are the roads safe enough for us to be able to leave if we so choose?" asked Jackson.

"In a word, no," the Sheriff said. "We have been getting bad reports over the last day and a half."

"What kind of reports?" asked Earl.

"Scavengers attacking vehicles on the highway."

"How about Islamists and Militia folks? How much trouble are we really in?" asked Jackson. "The truth, please."

"The Islamists? They took us by surprise here," the Sheriff said. "We were told they were all contained east of Flagstaff. We knew there were militia active between here and Tusayan. We had no idea they were working with the Islamists. That one is a shock, at least to me. I don't understand what is going on there. The objectives of these two groups don't coincide."

"Yes they do," Jackson said. "Just like the Venezuelans and the Islamists also lined up. They want to topple the US Government, or secede and set up their own territories. They want to appoint themselves warlords."

"Wonderful," Jerry said, walking out onto the veranda. "They are both pretty damn stupid. They have no chance of winning, but even if they did, as soon as they got the US authorities out of the way and the US citizens under control, they would be fighting each other. Idiots."

"I saw a story on TV last night about some Islamists that were caught sneaking over the Canadian border yesterday," said Earl. "The report said that a number of these creeps probably got through. Wonder if these Islamists are from the southeast or the north?"

"Another good reason not to get back on the road now," the Sheriff said.

Just then an Army Humvee drove in through the gate and parked in front of the clubhouse. There were two officers in the front, and four troops in the back. They all jumped out of the vehicle. The officers made their way towards the veranda.

"Who's in charge here?" asked the one of the officers.

{ 3 }

The Cavalry Arrives

The four soldiers that got out of the back of the Humvee stood around the vehicle with their weapons in their hands, keeping an eye on the crowd. The two officers were up on the veranda of the clubhouse.

"I asked who was in charge here?" the officer asked. He had a surly manner.

"I'm the owner of the park, sir," Hilda said. "But we don't have anyone formally in charge."

"That's going to change," he said.

"Actually, no it's not," Jerry said, stepping up. "We have information for you guys. We'll give it to you, and then you will be leaving us alone. This is still a free country, and we aren't under martial law here."

"And who are you?" asked the officer.

"A citizen, and a Marine," Jerry said. "My name is Jerry. Who are you?"

"Lieutenant James," the officer said. He was starting to calm down. "Where did you serve?"

"Gulf War," Jerry said.

The other officer whispered something in Lieutenant James's ear.

"Alright, sorry I came on so strong," he said. "Who can fill me in on what happened this morning?"

"Why don't you come into the clubhouse?" asked the Sheriff. "We can talk in there. All but one person involved in the action this morning are inside."

"Okay, fine," said the Lieutenant, and he and the other officer followed the Sheriff and Jerry. Hilda brought up the rear.

"Would you gentlemen like some coffee?" she asked.

"That would be great, thanks," said the Lieutenant. "Oh, and this is Major Hobbs."

"Have a seat, gentlemen," the Sheriff said. "We'll fill you in on what we know."

"Where's the other person involved?" asked Major Hobbs.

"He's out in a deer blind behind the RV Park, keeping watch," Jerry said. "That's where all the action happened this morning."

"Alright, we can talk to him later. Which of you were involved?"

Jeb, Jerry, the Sheriff, and Hilda raised their hands.

"What happened?" asked the Major.

"We were all sitting in here talking to the Sheriff about a death that happened last night," Jerry said.

"Death?" asked the Major.

"Yes," the Sheriff said. "A murder, we believe."

"Really?"

"Yeah, and the person who died was our ham radio operator," Jerry said. "More on that later, though. You want to hear about what happened this morning, correct?"

"Yes," the Major said. "Please go on."

"So anyway, we heard shots coming from the back of the park," Jerry said. "Sheriff Brown ran out there to see what was going on. He came back in a few seconds, and asked about the deer blinds in the back."

"Then my mom called on the cell phone," Jasmine said. "She was out in our rig, and she could hear Jeb calling for help. We couldn't hear it up here."

"I see," the Major said.

"Jerry and Frank went running back to the rear of the park, and they picked up their guns from their rigs on the way," the Sheriff said. "I went out there too."

"I take it Frank is the person who is back in the deer blind right now?" asked the Major.

"Yes," Jerry said.

"I probably should take it from here, guys, since I was out there. I'm Jeb."

"Alright," the Major said, looking back at Jeb as he hobbled over. "Were you wounded?"

"Yep, traitorous creep shot me in the leg. Just a flesh wound, though."

"He patched up just fine," the Doctor said from the back of the room.

"You the doctor?" asked the Major.

"Yes. By the way, that bullet was definitely military hardball. Passed clean through, no expansion."

"Interesting," the Major said. "Go on, Jeb."

"I spent the night up in the blind," Jeb said. "So I wake up at about 8:30 or so this morning. I hear voices, and the sound of some men coming towards the blind. I stood up and grabbed my rifle. Then I heard the shot, and felt the bullet go into my leg. I fell over, and pulled the door of the blind shut while I was laying there. Then I got up with my rifle and fired at the guy that shot me. Nailed him right in the head with my .270. Before these guys knew what was going on, I had three more down, but that was the end of my ammo. My Remington bolt action doesn't hold many rounds, and I wasn't carrying any extra."

"I see. So then you called for help, I take it?" asked the Major.

"Yep. Glad old Rosie heard me," he said.

"Who's Rosie?" asked the Major.

"That's my mom," Jasmine said.

"Good thing she's not here. She'd be all over you, Major. She likes men in uniform," Jerry said, laughing. Major Hobbs smiled.

"So the three of you went back behind the park with guns," the Major said. "What happened next?"

"Frank had his dog with him," Jerry said. "She's a Jack Russell. We went through the back gate and called out to Jeb. Then he yelled to look out, and somebody started shooting at us from the forest. We all hit the dirt. The Jack Russell saw where the shooter was, and Frank could see where she was looking, so he aimed his rifle in that direction. He saw some movement, and fired. He killed that one. We inched forward, and asked Jeb if he saw any other bad guys. He said no, so we continued, but then the dog started to growl and looked over at some bushes. This time I saw a person in the bushes, so I fired at them with my M-1 Carbine. I hit him a couple of times, but he got up and started running."

"Damn .30 Carbines are useless," Jeb said.

"Yeah," the Major said. "Did he get away?"

"No, Frank shot him with his Winchester," Jerry said.

"Oh, 30-30?" asked the Major.

"No, he's got a sweet little saddle gun in .44 Mag," Jeb said.

"Well, that will do the job," the Major said. "Any more?"

"Nope, that was it," the Sheriff said. "We don't know if there were others there that escaped, or if the entire party was just these six guys."

"Where are the bodies?" asked the Major.

"Right where they fell back there." the Sheriff said.

"Ok, anything else?" asked the Major.

"Yeah, three of them are Islamist fighters, and three of them are militia guys," Jerry said.

The Major looked over at the Lieutenant.

"Crap," said the Major. "We had heard a couple of reports that they were working together, but didn't believe it. Guess we have proof now. I'd like to take my men back there to investigate, and also to patrol the area to make sure nobody else is left. Could you call Frank and tell him we're on our way? I'd rather not get hit with a .44 mag today."

"I'll call him," Jane said. "I'm Frank's wife."

"Thank you," he said. "Jerry, you're welcome to come with us, and you too, Sheriff."

"I'll go if you need me," Jeb said.

"No you won't, hop along," said the Doctor. "Keep off that leg as much as you can for the next couple of days."

Jane got Frank on the phone.

"Frank?"

"Hi, honey," he said. "Everything alright up there?"

"Yes, we're fine. I'm not happy about you being out there by yourself."

"I know, but somebody had to stay, and I've got a lot of ammo on my belt. What's up?"

"The Army is here. Six men. They are coming back, with Jerry and the Sheriff. Just wanted to make sure you knew so you don't shoot them."

He laughed. "Alright, sounds good."

"Ok, they're leaving now. Love you," she said.

"Love you too, sweetheart."

Jane hung up and set down her cellphone.

"Okay, he knows you guys are coming," she said.

"Thanks," the Major said. "Lieutenant, got get the guys and we'll get moving."

"Roger that, sir," he said, and he went out the door and had a brief chat with the men.

The Major, Jerry, and the Sheriff walked out the door and headed to the back of the park. The rest of the men caught up with them about halfway back.

"Look sharp, men, and don't shoot at the person in the deer blind. He's a good guy," the Major said. "We could have either Islamist fighters or militia men or both back here. Keep your eyes open."

The men nodded.

"That the gate?" asked the Major.

"Yep," Jerry said. Jerry opened it, and all of the men went through. They walked about fifty yards.

"Frank," shouted Jerry.

"Yeah, Jerry, I see you guys."

"Any sign of more cretins?" He shouted.

"Nope, quiet as a church back here, but we have some vultures circling. Look up."

"Well, I'll be damned," Jerry said when he saw them. "That didn't take long.

"You sure there's no activity back here?" asked the Major.

"Who's that?" asked Frank.

"It's Major Hobbs, Frank," Jerry said.

"Oh. Yes, Major, I'm pretty sure, because I have my eyes and ears up here."

The Major gave Jerry and the Sheriff a quizzical look.

"He's talking about that Jack Russell of his," the Sheriff said. "That little sucker gave us a good warning earlier."

"Oh, I get it," said the Major.

"What now?" asked Jerry.

"How many people will that blind hold?" asked the Major.

"I think it ought to be able to hold four without any problem," Jerry said.

"Alright. Lieutenant, you take the troops back a little further and look around. I'm going up into the blind with these guys."

"Will do, Major," he said. "Alright you guys, let's go."

"Frank, we're coming up," Jerry said.

"Come on up and have a drink," Frank said. He laughed.

The Sheriff was first up the ladder, then the Major, and then Jerry.

"I can see why Jer used to brag about this thing," the Sheriff said with a grin. This is nice. I take it that cabinet has the stash."

"Who's Jer?" asked the Major.

"He was Hilda's husband," the Sheriff said. "And an old friend of mine. He passed a few years ago."

"Oh."

"Take a look at this," Frank said. He raised the top of the table, and showed off the booze and magazines.

"Dang, you weren't kidding about a drink," the Major said. He laughed.

"Hilda made Jer take all of the booze out of the house," the Sheriff said. "So he made himself this little retreat. It's not a bad deer blind, either, from what he said."

"This looks like ¾ inch marine grade plywood," the Major said. "Will take a decent sized bullet. A .50 cal would blow a hole through it, but it's going to stop a lot of small arm fire."

"Yep, and if it gets real bad, you might be able to hide behind one of the tree trunks," Frank said. "That being said, this is no fort. Bad place to get trapped in. It's a good lookout though."

"Well, we need to talk, gentlemen," the Major said.

"I figured," Frank said. "I miss anything at the clubhouse?"

"Not a lot," Jerry said.

"We had been hearing rumors that the Islamists and the militia were working together," Major Hobbs said. "This is the first time we've seen proof."

"How much trouble are they going to give the military?" asked Frank.

"Oh, we'll take care of them, but we're still fighting the Islamists over by Flagstaff, and trying to mop up around Phoenix. Tucson is pretty well locked down, and so is Yuma. The bigger problem is down in Mexico."

"I had a feeling that was going to be the case," Frank said. "Are we going to annex Mexico?"

"No, not exactly," the Major said. "We have basically merged with Mexico. The majority of the people down there are for it now. It's going to take a lot of time and resources to rid the area of Mexican Nationalist forces and the Islamists. The Islamists got stuck there when we shut down our borders and blew the shit out of Venezuela."

"Don't tell me, let me guess," Jerry said. "The Islamists south of the border are allied with the Mexican Nationalists, and that's working so good for them that they decided to try the same thing here."

"That's what it sounds like to me," the Major said. "And of course we don't have enough troops to cover everything. Luckily the Mexican army is with us down south, and they didn't get hit with nukes, so their population is intact."

"Can you tell us anything about the Canadian border?" asked Frank. "We've heard that there have been Islamists coming down through there."

"Yes, I have intelligence saying the same thing," the Major said. "Not a good situation. If it wasn't for that, I'd advise you folks to move north. You still can, but I wouldn't go above Wyoming at this point."

"How are things back east?" asked Jerry.

"Better than out here, actually," the Major said, "the problem is getting there. You don't want to go through New Mexico, that's for sure. And there is more than just the enemy to worry about."

"You mean the scavengers I've heard about, I suspect," said the Sheriff. "I've been trying to talk these folks into staying here because

Bug Out! Part 3 – Motorhome Madness

of them. And that was before we heard anything about Islamists coming down from Canada."

"Well, depending on how powerful the enemy is in this area, that might be the best advice," the Major said. "We need to find out if these folks here were a scouting party, or the sign of a major movement into this area. If it's a major movement, you might have no choice but to hit the road."

"If it was a scouting party looking for supplies and we killed all of them off, we might be alright," the Sheriff said.

"We need to see if we can find their vehicle," Jerry said. "There's a place to park back by the highway. If there's no vehicle there, we need to assume that some of them may have gotten away."

"Exactly," the Major said. "Want to show us where this parking area is?"

"Sure, no problem," Jerry said.

"Want me to stay up here?" asked Frank.

"Sure, just don't get trigger happy," the Major said.

"You got it," Frank replied.

"Let me radio the Lieutenant to let him know we're going back there," Major Hobbs said. He pulled out a small radio and called him. "Lieutenant, we're coming down to take a look at a parking area by the highway. We want to see if there's a car there or not."

"Roger that," he replied. "That will tell us if there were only six."

"Got it, Hobbs out."

The Sheriff, Jerry, and Major Hobbs all climbed down the ladder and headed carefully towards the parking area.

Meanwhile, back at the clubhouse, Hilda was serving up coffee and trying to keep people calm. Jasmine went back to her rig to get Rosie, and they slowly made their way in through the door.

"Good morning, all," she said. "Mimosas?"

"Mom, I don't think you should start drinking this early."

"Why not?"

{ 35 }

"What if we have to leave in a hurry?"

"Ok," she said. "Guess I'll have coffee."

"I'll go get you some, mom. Sit down here, I'm sure there's some good conversation." Jasmine went over to the coffee pot and filled two cups. She brought them over and handed one to Rosie.

"Thank you, daughter," Rosie said.

"How are you today, Rosie?" asked Jane.

"I have slight hangover, but ok," she said. "How you?"

"We'll, I'd be better if we didn't have problems behind the park," Jane said.

"Frank okey doke?" she asked.

"So far. Jerry too. The army is back there now," Jane said.

"I trust Jerry more than army," Rosie said.

"Yes, Jerry and Frank did well today," Jane said.

"And the Sheriff," Hilda said, walking over. "I'm going to take a cup of coffee up to Charlie. And a bottle of water or two. It's going to get hot up there later."

"Where Charlie?" asked Rosie.

"He's got lookout duty on top of the store," Hilda said.

"Oh. He good man," Rosie said.

"Yes, he is, Rosie," Hilda said. "I'll be back in a little while."

Hilda went into the store and through the door into the store room. She climbed the steps up to the roof, and went out.

"Hi, sweetie, brought you some coffee," Hilda said.

"Ah, perfect," Charlie said. He smiled at her as she handed him the cup.

"Here's a couple bottles of water, too," she said.

"What's going on down there?"

"The army is looking around down by the blinds."

"Good," Charlie said. "This is going to get our people working together, but I got out of there so I wouldn't come on too strong again."

"You didn't come on too strong, Charlie," Hilda said. "Sometimes people need to figure out what's right on their own. Remember that these folks were taken for a ride by some pretty bad element before you met them."

"Yeah, I know," Charlie said. "They are all good folks, too. We're lucky they showed up. It could have been a lot worse."

"I know. I had such a nice time at Happy Hour, until the thing happened with Arthur."

"Did the Army ask about him?"

"No, they didn't know," Hilda said, "until we brought it up."

"Oh. I just figured that the Sheriff would have brought it up."

"I don't think he talked to them until the fire fight happened this morning."

"Alright," Charlie said. "Are any of the guests making noise like they want to leave?"

"A few, but the Sheriff is still saying that the road is too dangerous, and then we have those reports of Islamists coming down from Canada. But you never know what's going to happen. If it's obvious that we have more trouble coming here, we all may be leaving."

"True." Charlie turned and looked out into the distance in front of the park. He took a sip of his coffee, and Hilda came up alongside him. She put his arm around his waist, and he put his arm on her shoulder.

Back behind the park Jerry, Major Hobbs, and the Sheriff made it over the creek and into the flat meadow that was used as a parking spot. There was a beat up old Suburban sitting there. The Sheriff started to double time it over.

"Sheriff, don't walk around there carelessly," Jerry shouted. "We need to check for tire tracks around it."

"You're right," he said, and he slowed down until the other two men caught up.

Looks like a militia vehicle to me," Major Hobbs said.

"Yeah, sure does," the Sheriff said.

"Look at those tire tracks next to it. Those are fresh," Jerry said. "And look at those drops of blood."

{ 4 }

On the Run

Jerry, the Sheriff, and Major Hobbs looked down at the fresh tire tracks, and the spots of blood next to them.

"Well, It's pretty obvious at least one man escaped that fire fight," Major Hobbs said.

"Let's follow the tracks to the highway. Maybe we can tell what direction they took off," Jerry said.

The other two men nodded, and they followed Jerry as he tracked the fresh tread marks. They could follow them plainly all the way to the road.

"Looks like they turned left," Jerry said, looking at the Sheriff. "What's over there?"

"A few ranches, and then wilderness for a lot of miles," the Sheriff said.

"So if we're lucky, whoever escaped didn't really know where they were going. If the driver was wounded badly, we may find him up the highway," Jerry said.

"Alright, I'm going to call my troops back to the park, and we'll get in our unit and follow the road in that direction," the Major said. "Maybe we'll get lucky. Sheriff, can you lead us from the front of the RV Park to this piece of road?"

"Sure thing, Major," the Sheriff said.

"Wait a minute, before you guys dash off," Jerry said. "This little parking area is only known by locals. These guys knew to come here in order to sneak into the RV Park. Whoever killed Arthur probably called them, and they're probably still with us. How are we going to figure out who?"

"That's a damn good question, Jerry," Major Hobbs said. "Any suggestions, Sheriff?"

"I was here to do some interviews this morning, after we determined that Arthur was murdered," the Sheriff said. "I was just starting that when we heard the shots fired."

"I'll tell you what, then," Major Hobbs said. "After you get us out here, why don't you go back to that? If we don't figure out who the mole is, we're going to have a big problem."

"Agreed."

"I think I'll go up and keep Frank company for a while," Jerry said.

"Got it," Major Hobbs said. He pulled out his radio. "Lieutenant?"

"Roger."

"Meet me back at the RV Park. We need to get in the Humvee and follow the highway. Looks like at least one person escaped from the fire fight. You see anything back here?"

"Well, we found a lot of fresh footprints. We were just following some that appear to be leading to the front part of the park."

"How fresh?"

"I'd say this morning," the Lieutenant answered.

"Good, follow those through to the end if you can. If the footsteps lead to a motor home, make note of which one it is, but don't do anything. Meet me back at the clubhouse when you are done."

The Major put his radio in his pocked.

"Alright, you guys heard that. Let's go back to the clubhouse."

The three men walked back across the creek, and over to the blind.

"Frank," Jerry shouted. "I'm coming up."

"Alright," Frank said. Jerry put his carbine on his back with the sling and climbed up, as the Major and the Sheriff continued on to the gate.

"Well, what happened?" asked Frank.

"There was an old Suburban parked back there. Looks like a militia vehicle."

"How can you tell?"

"It just screamed redneck, for one thing," Jerry said. Both men cracked up.

"Interesting. Good that it's still there, that probably means we got them all."

"Nope. There were fresh tire tracks right next to it, and there were drops of blood on the ground. Somebody got away."

"Shit. What now?"

"The Lieutenant saw some fresh foot tracks that appear to be leading from back here into the front half of the park. He's tracking those with the rest of the troops."

"Interesting," Frank said. "I was thinking that somebody inside must have tipped off these scumbags. Otherwise how would they know about us? How would they know somebody was in the blind?"

"Yeah, I could see them coming to the front of the park, but how did they know about that parking area back there, and the trail over the creek?"

Frank nodded at Jerry.

"Yep, I'm guessing whoever killed Arthur also called these folks in."

"Fraid so," Jerry said. "The Major knows it too. He asked the Sheriff to lead them to the highway by the parking area so they can follow in the direction that the second car went. Then he told the Sheriff to come back and continue to investigate the murder of Arthur."

"That Major is sharp. The Sheriff.....not so much."

{41}

"Yeah, you got that right. That Sheriff is as dumb as a box of rocks. Probably no problem when all he had to do was keep rowdy campers under control."

"Yeah," Frank said. "And his partner reminds me of Barney Fife." Both men cracked up again.

"I wish Jeb wasn't hurt. He's the only other good man we've got."

"We should patch things up with Charlie if we are going to stick around."

"I agree," Jerry said. "How about Jackson and Earl?"

"I don't trust them anymore," Frank said. "Somebody is the mole. Might be one of them."

"Could be. They were asking more questions than anybody else this morning when the Sheriff was briefing people on the fire fight."

"Really? That's interesting. We shouldn't jump to any conclusions yet, though. Could be somebody else."

"Agreed," Jerry said. "How much booze is left?"

"A lot."

"Good thing Rosie can't get up here," Jerry said, cracking up once again.

"Yeah, she's a card. I can see why you like her so much. She's the life of the party."

"Yep. Jasmine tries to keep her in line. It's funny to watch."

"I take it you two don't have any kids?"

"Nope, we got married a little too late for that. Second time around for me."

"Where did you guys meet?"

"Work. Jasmine is pretty sharp, by the way."

"I can tell."

Franks phone rang. He answered it.

"Frank?" asked Jane.

"Yes, sweetie. What's up?"

"Just wondering how much longer you are going to be out there."

"Oh, probably not too much longer. I'm sure Lucy needs to get down and do some business, for one thing."

"You alone?"

"No, Jerry is up here now."

"Good. The Sheriff just took off with the Army guys, to show them how to get back to road by the parking area."

"Did the Lieutenant say anything about the footsteps?"

"What footsteps?"

"Well, I guess not," Frank said. "Apparently there were some fresh footsteps back here that looked like they came from the front part of the park. The Lieutenant and the four men found them. Major Hobbs told them to continue to track."

Jerry got his attention.

"Just a sec, honey," Frank said. "What?"

"Tell her not to say anything about the footsteps to anybody at the park," Jerry said. "The Major didn't want his guys to do anything if they led to a motor home."

"You hear that, Sweetie?"

"Yes," Jane said. "Understand, I'll keep quiet."

"How are things going down there?"

"Well, the clubhouse is more fun now that Rosie is here."

Frank laughed.

"Yeah, Jerry and I were just talking about her. What's going on with Charlie?"

"He's still on watch, on the roof of the store. Hilda has been up there with him for a little while. She was taking him some coffee."

"OK. I won't be too much longer, I promise."

"Bye, honey. I love you."

"Love you too," Frank said. He put his phone in his pocket.

"Sounds like Rosie is doing what she does best," Jerry said.

"Yeah, sounds like."

"If you want to go down, no problem. I'll stick around up here."

"Maybe in a little while. I'd rather wait until the Sheriff gets back, at least."

"Alright," Jerry said.

Back at the clubhouse, Hilda was just walking back in.

"Hi, all," Hilda said. "How's the coffee holding up?"

"We still have plenty," Jane said. "How's Charlie doing?"

"He's fine. There hasn't been much traffic on the road so far. What did the Major say before he left?"

"They found an old Suburban in the parking area, but there were also fresh tire tracks next to it, and a few drops of blood on the ground."

Hilda got a sick look on her face.

"That means somebody escaped," she said. "That's not good."

"Yep. The Major took his folks and went around to see if they could find the vehicle. It looks like it turned left on the highway."

"Left, huh?" Hilda said. "Nothing back there other than a couple of ranches, and a lot of desert. Good way to get north, though."

"Well, the Major is hoping that the person driving was wounded badly enough to have passed out down the road."

"When Jerry come back?" asked Rosie, as she was walking up to them.

"Shouldn't be too much longer," Jane said. "I just talked to Frank on the phone. Jerry is up in the blind with him now."

"Oh, that blind with booze?" she said, grinning.

Jane shook her head and laughed.

"Yes, that blind with the booze. And don't forget the girly magazines."

"Jerry not need girly magazines. He has my daughter. She better."

"Oh, yes, I'm sure of that," Jane said. She glanced over at Hilda, and all three ladies laughed.

"You keep Charlie warm at night?" Rosie asked, looking at Hilda. She got an embarrassed smile, and her face turned red.

"Well, I guess it's really no secret," Hilda said. "Charlie and I are together. We used to date in High School, by the way."

"Really. But you married other man later?" asked Rosie.

"Yes, I married Jer instead. And Charlie married another lady. Both are gone now, so why not get together?"

"That good," Rosie said. "Wish I could have old boyfriend now. He in Philippines. Maybe not alive anymore."

"I know I'm lucky," Hilda said. "I feel like a kid again."

The Sheriff's car drove up in front of the clubhouse. The Sheriff got out, and he had his deputy with him this time.

"Well, the Major is hot on the trail of that other car now," the Sheriff said. "I need to continue my investigation on Arthur."

"Good," Jane said. "We need to figure that out."

"Can you call Frank and Jerry, please?" I'll send the Deputy back there to man the blind."

"Sure, no problem," Jane said. She pulled out her cellphone.

"Frank?"

"Hi, honey," he said.

"The Sheriff is back, and wants to continue the investigation on Arthur's death. Could you and Jerry come back here? The Deputy is coming out to take over in the blind."

"Sure, we could use a break. We'll come after the Deputy gets here."

Jane hung up the phone.

"Alright, Sheriff, they'll come back here after the Deputy gets out there."

"Great, thank you," he said. "Deputy, go on back, and take the rifle that I put in the trunk, with some ammo."

"No problem," he said as he was leaving. "I'll radio you if I see anything."

"Any more of that coffee left, Hilda?" asked the Sheriff.

"Sure, help yourself," she said. "You want Jeb back here? He went back to his rig to sleep for a while."

"Later," he said. "The Doc left, I take it?"

"Yeah, he took off about the same time that the Major left."

"Alright."

Frank and Jerry walked through the door after about five minutes. They walked over to the Sheriff.

"Sheriff, maybe we should talk somewhere more private," Jerry said.

You guys can use my office," Hilda said. "It's that door back in the rear of the room, next to the stage."

"Thanks, Hilda," the Sheriff said. "Let's go."

The three men walked back to the office door. The Sheriff opened it and ushered Jerry and Frank in."

"Have a seat, guys," the Sheriff said. Everybody sat down.

"Where'd the footprints lead?" asked Frank.

"Well, they definitely led into the park, through the side gate up towards the front, but after they got in a little ways, they were pretty well wiped out by other foot traffic from this morning."

"Who did the tracking?" asked Jerry.

"The Lieutenant."

"Hmmmm, wonder if he's any good at tracking? Extra foot traffic makes it harder, but it's not impossible if there is a good pattern from the prints."

"You want to go out and give it a shot?" asked the Sheriff.

"Not now. If the bad guys are still around, they would see me looking."

"You think they might have left?"

"Well, it is possible," Frank said. "They have to know that the heat is on."

"Well, let's drop this part and focus on Arthur," the Sheriff said.

Frank and Jerry looked at each other.

"You know that whoever killed Arthur probably called the scumbags that we fought this morning, correct?" asked Jerry.

"What makes you think that?" asked the Sheriff.

Frank and Jerry looked at each other again.

"Sheriff, somebody here had to have called them. They knew where that parking area was, and the trail over the creek. They knew where the blind was too. They got the drop on Jeb, and I'll bet that isn't easy to do."

The Sheriff sat there looking at the two men. You could see the gears in his head turning.

"Okay, I think you probably have something there," he said. "So what now?"

"We need to interview anybody who wasn't at Happy Hour the last night," Frank said.

"Do you know who wasn't there?" asked the Sheriff.

"Off the top of my head, I know of some," Frank said. "And I know of some people who were gone during parts of the evening."

"Me too, but it might help to have Hilda in here to help us remember everybody," Jerry said.

"Alright, I'll go get her," the Sheriff said.

"Wait a minute," Jerry said. "Did the coroner tell you how long Arthur had been dead?"

"He gave me a range. Between four and sixteen hours. But remember that he didn't start looking at the body until a couple hours after they picked it up."

Jerry and Frank looked at each other again.

"We can't count on this happening during Happy Hour," Frank said.

"I was thinking it would have been difficult for this to have happened during broad daylight," mused Jerry. "I'm changing my mind. The person or persons who did this were brazen enough to pull that off easily."

"So did you see Arthur hanging around with anybody in particular?" asked the Sheriff.

"No....huh.....wait," Jerry said. "Cynthia was in his rig with him."

"You don't think that little lady could have killed Arthur, do you?" asked the Sheriff.

"Arthur was a very frail old man," Jerry said. "Hell, he probably didn't weigh much over a hundred pounds. Yeah, she could have easily killed him."

"Jerry's right," Frank said. "We can place her there during the time in question. Maybe we should bring her back in."

"Alright, you two," said the Sheriff. "Not sure that I agree here, but I'll go talk to Hilda. I'll have her go get Cynthia, and then they can both come in here." He got up and left the room.

"We are going to have to lead this character through every step of this investigation. You know that, right?" asked Jerry.

"Sad. I wonder if he has any criminal investigators on his force."

"Well, there's always Barney," Jerry said. The two men cracked up again.

Jane poked her head through the door.

"What's going on?" she asked.

"The Sheriff went out to get Hilda and Cynthia back here," Frank said. "How's it going out there?"

"Rosie is keeping us entertained. She's already asking when Happy Hour is." Jane smirked.

"That's my girl," Jerry said. "Jasmine still here?"

"Yes, she's been sitting by the window reading her Kindle most of the time."

"Sounds about right," Jerry said. "It drives her nuts to watch her mom being the life of the party."

"Here comes the Sheriff," Jane said. "Talk to you later, sweetie. Bye, Jerry."

Both men nodded. The Sheriff came back in.

"Alright, Hilda went to get Cynthia. She'll be back in a couple of minutes. Where were we?"

"Well, when the murder could have happened," Frank said. "And who do we know of that had access to Arthur....Either during Happy Hour or before?"

"Yeah, that covers it," Jerry said.

Hilda rushed into the office.

"Cynthia is gone," Hilda said, sounding out of breath.

"No, really?" asked the Sheriff. "Is her rig still here?"

"Yes, but her car is gone. And Jerry, the door of your coach is hanging open. I saw it on the way back."

Jerry looked at Frank, eyes wide open.

"The radio," Jerry said. He got out of his chair and took off running.

"I'll call Charlie and see what time he saw her leave," Hilda said. She pulled her cellphone out of her pocket.

"Charlie?"

"Yes, Hilda, what's up?" Charlie asked.

"Did you see any cars leave the park?"

"Yes, I saw a Honda CRV leave about an hour ago. Didn't think anything of it. Why."

"I was just down looking for Cynthia. She's gone. Her coach was left open."

"Uh Oh," Charlie said.

Just then Jerry ran back into the office.

"The radio's gone," he said, trying to catch his breath.

"I think our murder investigation is over, Sheriff," Frank said.

"What's happening?" asked Charlie over the phone.

"Looks like Cynthia took off with the short wave radio. She broke into Jerry's rig and took it on the way out."

"Crap. Never would have pegged her as the one," Charlie said.

Suddenly there was a pop, pop, pop in the distance.

"Did you guys hear that?" asked Charlie.

"Yes," Hilda said.

"I know that sound," Jerry said. "Gunfire, about half a mile away."

Then there was more. Pop pop pop pop, muffled by the distance, and then two explosions.

"Grenades," Jerry said.

{ 5 }

Guns in the Distance

More distant gunfire. The muffled pop pop pop sound. Lucy looked towards the windows and growled.

"I can see some smoke," Charlie said over the cellphone to Hilda. She took the phone away from her ear.

"Charlie can see some smoke."

"Maybe we should all go up there to continue our meeting, so Charlie can be involved, and so we can see what's going on," Frank said.

Hilda nodded.

"Charlie, we're coming up."

"Great, see you in a few minutes."

Another pop pop pop, and two more loud explosions. Then more pop pop pop. It was starting to go faster now….too fast to count.

"That's more than just six guys shooting at a couple of militia nuts," Jerry said.

"Yeah, there's a fire fight going on down there," Frank said. "I hope the Major and his men didn't get ambushed."

"Me too," the Sheriff said. As they were walking towards the store, Earl and Jackson joined them.

"You guys are obviously hearing this," Earl said.

"C'mon, we're going up on the roof of the store to have a meeting," Frank said. He looked over at Jerry for approval, and he nodded. When they were almost to the door, Jane rushed over and got beside Frank. She looked up at him, and he put his arm around her shoulders. They walked into the store, and over to the back room door.

"Alright, everybody watch your step," Hilda said. They went into the dark storeroom, and Hilda turned on the lights. There was a rough wooden staircase in the back of the room, leading to a trap door. Hilda climbed up and pushed the trap door open. All of them walked up onto the roof.....Hilda followed by Frank and Jane, Jerry, the Sheriff, Earl, and Jackson. Jane carried Lucy up. Charlie was over at the edge of the flat roof, behind a façade that was about chest high. He was sitting on a short stool with a rifle in his hands.

"I know it's a little dirty, but you folks probably should sit down," Charlie said. "If you stand up and there are bad guys out there, they could hit you with a sniper rifle."

"Good point," Jerry said. He sat down Indian-style, and the others joined him.

"OK, so here's the situation as we know it right now," Frank said. "Major Hobbs took his troops and headed down the back highway, looking for the missing vehicle. Sheriff, is that billow of smoke over there in the direction that the highway leads?"

"Sure is," the Sheriff said.

"I figured. Sounds like whatever went on there is over, because it's been a couple of minutes since we've heard anything."

"That smoke looks like a vehicle fire to me," Jerry said.

"Just what I was thinking," Charlie said, looking back at the group. Then he turned back out to overlook the front of the park. Hilda went over and sat next to him.

"We also think we know who killed Arthur. It appears to have been Cynthia, and when she took off, she stole Arthur's short wave radio from Jerry's coach."

"Cynthia, huh?" asked Jackson. "Shoot. I should have seen that coming."

"What?" asked Jerry.

"Cynthia was very close to the leader of the militia," Jackson said.

"Close, hell, they were lovers," Earl said. "They had a big fight right before we left the militia, and she decided to go with us. Phony baloney. She fooled us good."

"Who's the leader of the militia?"

"Some nutcase named Franklin J. Hornady. And don't leave out the J or call him Frank. He don't like that." Earl looked over at Jackson, and they both laughed sarcastically. "That cretin is a legend in his own mind."

"Is he the brains of the operation?" asked Frank.

"No, that was Hank and Lewis," Jackson said. "Franklin J. Hornady is a charismatic character, though. He's probably the main thing holding that band of rednecks together now."

"Apparently he's made some kind of alliance with the Islamists. Half of the folks that we killed this morning were Islamists, the other half were militia men."

Earl and Jackson both laughed sarcastically again.

"Yeah, that sounds like Franklin," Earl said. "He never thinks things through past the first move. Hank and Lewis would have vetoed that for sure. As soon as the Islamists accomplish whatever objective they have, they will just behead all of those militia folks. Idiot."

"Tell us more about Cynthia," asked Charlie.

"She comes off all meek most of the time," Earl said. "She was always nice to me, but she also always made me a little nervous. I wasn't thrilled when she was coming with us."

"Did she really have a son in South Korea?"

"Yes, that part is true," Jackson said. "I actually know him. I think he joined the service to get away from his mom and Franklin."

"Franklin isn't the dad?" asked Jerry.

"No, she probably doesn't even know who his dad was," Earl said. "She was quite a looker back in the day. Wild gal. Real disco queen. Must have been hell to deal with as a mom. She can still pretty herself up enough to catch the attention of men, though. Worked on Franklin. Hell, I've even given her a second look myself."

"She just looked like an older mom to me," Frank said.

"She doesn't dress up that often," Jackson snorted. "Usually only when she wants something from somebody. She can be a good actress."

"I wish you guys would have mentioned this before now," Jerry said. "How come you weren't at Happy Hour last night?"

"We both had to quit drinking," Jackson said. "I'll bet you guys thought that Earl and I did in Arthur."

"Well, it did cross our minds," Frank said.

"Can't blame you for that, I guess," Earl said. "We'll take off if you don't trust us."

"No, don't do that," Frank said. "We're cool. We know who did it now. We could use able-bodied men at this point too, and you guys know more about the militia than anyone else here."

"Good, we'd like to stay," Jackson said. "Too many bad people out on the road."

"That brings us to the main thing we need to talk about. Do we make a stand here, or do we hi-tail it," Jerry said. "I don't think we'll know for sure what to do until the Major gets back here."

"If he gets back here," Frank said.

"Yeah," Jerry said. "This place does have some advantages for defense, but it could also turn into the Alamo."

"I still think you would be a lot less safe on the road," the Sheriff said. "You were going to go north. You might have gone up the same road the Major and his troops went up. Somebody was lighting off grenades up there. Could have been the Major, but it also could have been the bad guys."

"There's definitely some truth in what you are saying," Frank said. "This place is of no real strategic value that I can think of."

"Franklin J. Hornady is not a strategic thinker," Jackson said. "If he's coming here, it's to find the folks who killed Hank and Ken."

"Didn't Lewis just get arrested, not killed?" Frank asked. "What if he's out now and he rejoins the militia?"

"That wouldn't be good," Earl said. "But I'd be surprised if he's out. If he was, I doubt that the Williams Militia would be teaming up with Islamists. He'd know better."

"Yeah, I'd have to agree with Earl on that," Jackson said.

"How many people are left in the militia?" asked the Sheriff.

"Good question," Earl said. "There were a lot of 'casual' members who wouldn't have gone along with crap like this. At the peak, there were about sixty people in that group. I'd be a little surprised if they had half that now."

"I'm not sure I agree, Earl," Jackson said. "Things are crazy now, and Franklin might have many of them convinced that going it alone is more dangerous than staying with the group, even if they aren't on board with all of the decision making."

"Wonder if Officer Simmons is still in this mix?" asked Jane.

"If we're lucky the Islamists have already taken him out," Charlie said. He looked down at Hilda, then back at the group. "Bottom line here, in my way of thinking, is that we need to be able to carefully compare the relative safety of being on the road vs. staying here. I don't think we have enough info to do that yet."

"Yeah, I agree, that is the basic problem," Frank said. "And as much as I hate to go there, if it does turn out that we need to make a stand, we're going to have to get better organized, or somebody is going to get the drop on us."

Frank looked over at Jerry, and he nodded back at Frank.

"It's been quiet for quite a while," the Sheriff said. "If things went well, the Major ought to be back before too long."

"Hopefully we won't see the other side come back through here," Jane said. Hilda looked at her and nodded.

"You heard from your deputy lately, Sheriff?" asked Jerry.

"No, as a matter of fact," he replied. "I'd better go radio him." He got up and went downstairs, and out to his patrol car.

"That Sheriff is a little passive, isn't he?" asked Jackson.

"Yes, bless his heart, he's no leader," Hilda said. "Nice enough guy, and he's always here quickly when I need him, but this world is way beyond his capability."

"Yeah, Jerry and I were talking about that too," Frank said. "We'll need to fill in for him at times. At least he's not one of those proud types who wants control even if he can't handle it."

"He's a real good shot with a long gun," Charlie said. "As good as Jeb."

"He didn't even fire off a shot in that altercation we had this morning," Jerry said. "And he only brought his handgun."

"Yeah, good at shooting a gun and good in a fight are two different things," Jackson said.

"Hey, I can't get an answer from the Deputy," shouted the Sheriff from the parking lot next to the store. "I'd better go out there and check on him."

The other men leapt to their feet.

"Wait for us, Sheriff, we're coming too," Frank shouted. "And get your shotgun this time."

"Okay," he shouted back.

"Hilda and Jane, want to hold the fort up here?" asked Charlie.

"Sure," Hilda said. "I'm not a bad shot myself. How about you, Jane?"

"I can shoot," she said, looking nervously over at Frank. "Don't you go getting yourself killed back there. Take Lucy."

{56}

"I'll be fine, honey," Frank replied, grabbing Lucy's leash. "Keep a good eye out here. If anything is going on, they might try to surround us. Wish we had Jeb up here with you girls."

"Stop by his rig and ask him to come over," Hilda said. "He'll come. He's not hurt that bad, and the stairs aren't that difficult."

"Alright, we'll do that," Frank said. They all went down the stairs.

"You two might want to stop by your rigs and get weapons," Jerry said to Jackson and Earl.

"Way ahead of you, buddy," Earl said grimly. Jackson nodded.

The men got to the Sheriff, who was pulling the shotgun off of its holder in the patrol car.

"Good, you brought the dog," the Sheriff said as he closed the car door. He looked at Jackson and Earl. "You two got rifles?"

"Yep, we're going to get them now," Earl said. They trotted off to their coaches, which were next to each other. Both came out with bolt action hunting rifles. Earl was emptying a box of ammo into his hands and stuffing rounds into his shirt pockets.

"There's Jeb's rig, I'll go over," Frank said. He went over and knocked on the door.

"It's open," Jeb said. Frank pushed the door open. Jeb was getting dressed.

"Heard the gunfire, huh?" asked Frank.

"Yep, figured you needed me."

"Could you go up on the roof of the store and help Hilda and Jane while we're in the back? We can't raise the Deputy that's in the blind."

"Sure, I'll do that," he said. "And I have a whole box of .270 rounds with me this time."

"Excellent. See you in a little while."

Frank rejoined the men.

"He going?" asked Jerry.

"Yeah, he already was getting dressed when I got there. He heard the gunfire."

"I'm going to call Jasmine and tell her to stay in the clubhouse. Our rig is too close to the back." He pulled out his phone and dialed as they were walking.

"Jasmine?"

"Where are you?"

"On my way back to the blind. We lost contact with the Deputy up there."

"Who's with you?"

"Frank, the Sheriff, Charlie, Jackson, and Earl."

"Good. Be careful back there."

"Will do. You and Rosie stay in the clubhouse, OK?"

"Sure, no problem," she said.

"Alright, talk to you later," he said. "Love you."

"Love you too, honey. Don't get shot."

Jerry put his phone back in his pocket.

"Happy Hour might be a little late tonight," Frank said. "Hope Rosie takes it OK." Jerry, the Sheriff, and Charlie all cracked up. Earl and Jackson gave them a quizzical look.

"My mother-in-law," Jerry said to them. "She likes to party."

"Oh," Earl said.

"What are you guys packing?" asked Jerry.

"I've got an old Remington bolt action 30-06," Earl said.

"Mine's a .270 Winchester bolt," Jackson said.

"Good stuff," Jerry said. "Guess I'm low man again with this damn .30 Carbine."

"There's the gate, let's cut the chatter," the Sheriff said. The men hushed up and crept forward, slipping through the gate. Frank took off Lucy's leash and hung it on the fence. In another 20 yards they saw the blind. They made their way as quietly as they could. They could barely see the trees that the blind was in. Lucy started to growl. The men hit the dirt and crawled up behind some bushes. They couldn't see the blind yet, only higher up on the trees.

"Split up," Jerry whispered. "Two over there, two on the other side, two in the middle."

They fanned out and continued to move forward. Frank and Jerry were in the center, with the Sheriff and Charlie to the left and Earl and Jackson to the right.

A low growl, and Lucy stopped walking. Frank could just see the blind now. There was a man dressed in black climbing the ladder. Frank got a bead on him with the Winchester and fired. The man flew off the ladder. Frank moved the lever to reload the Winchester. Then several shots came their way. They hit the dirt. Lucy looked over to the left. Frank and Jerry both saw a man dressed in black get up and start running towards them. Both Frank and Jerry got him in their sights, but before they could shoot his head exploded.

"Charlie, I'll bet," Frank whispered. "The sheriff just has a scatter gun. That was a big rifle round."

They went forward a little further, and Lucy growled again. She looked towards some bushes by the trees opposite of the blind. Frank saw movement again. He aimed and fired. He saw another man roll out of the bushes and then get up to run. This man had a camo suit on. He got about three steps before he got shot square in the back, hard enough to throw him forward. Frank and Jerry looked over, and saw Earl work the bolt on his 30-06 to chamber another round. Then there was silence, for a few minutes. All of the men were afraid to get up, so they watched and listened. Lucy was quiet. Then the Sheriff shouted.

"Terry, you up there?"

"Yeah, Sheriff, but I'm scared," he shouted, sounding ashamed. "I couldn't bring myself to fire."

"You aren't hit?" asked Jerry.

"No," he said.

"Alright," the Sheriff said. "I'm coming up. Sit tight, and keep your eyes open."

"Sure that's a good idea, Sheriff?" asked Jerry. "You might make a really good target. If they get a bead on you, we aren't giving up to save you."

"Yeah, don't, because they'll just kill us all anyway," he said. "I have to go up. That's my nephew."

"Understand," Jerry said.

There was a rustle, and the Sheriff emerged from the bushes, crouching, and tried to make his way to the ladder. Then a shot went off. It missed, and the Sheriff hit the dirt. Frank saw where the shot came from and pointed over at it, then looked at Jerry, who smiled and aimed the .30 carbine in that direction. He flutter-triggered it, causing about 10 rounds from the 30 round magazine to fire in rapid succession. Somebody cried out, and rolled into sight. Earl nailed him with the 30-06.

"Another militia guy," said Charlie, who could see him lying in the dirt.

The Sheriff got up again, and made his way to the ladder. He climbed up like his life depended on it, and jumped in.

"He okay?" called Frank.

"Yeah, just shook up. I'm going to take a good look around with my field glasses. If I see anything, I'll use clock speak, with 12 O'clock high being right out the front door of the blind."

"Good idea," said Jerry. "That scattergun won't do much up there unless the bad guy is really close."

"Nothing between 9 O'clock and 12 O'clock that I can see. Not that much cover over there."

"Good."

"Lots of cover between 12 O'clock and 3 O'clock. Can't see in there very well."

Charlie scurried over to where Frank and Jerry were.

Bug Out! Part 3 – Motorhome Madness

"I'm going over to the parking area. If there's a vehicle there, I'll knife the tires."

"I'll go with you," Jerry said. "Damn good idea."

"I'll keep watch here with the police dog," Frank said. "Better sneak by Earl and Jackson, though, so they don't take a shot at you."

"Yeah, it's on the way anyhow," Charlie said. They snuck over there.

"Earl and Jackson, heads up," Charlie said. "We're coming over."

"Come ahead," Jackson said.

"We're going to go see if there's a vehicle in the parking area, and if there is, we're going to slash the tires."

"Good plan. We'll cover you," Earl said.

"Thanks, guys," Charlie said. He and Jerry crept slowly forward, following the creek. They made it to the crossover in minutes, and soon they were moving slowly down the pathway to the parking area. An old pickup truck sat in the parking lot.

Jerry touched Charlie's back. He turned, and Jerry got close and whispered.

"Look, I see feet behind the back side of that truck bed," Jerry said.

"Wow," Charlie said. "Good eyes. I see him now."

"I'll go around the right and see if I can get the drop on him," Jerry said. He slowly moved over.

Then there was the sound of a rifle cocking.

"Hold it right there, friends," said a voice from behind some bushes.

{ 6 }

Body Disposal

Jerry and Charlie froze, hearing the man approach them from behind.

"Drop the guns," he said in a gruff voice. Jerry and Charlie looked at each other. They both put their guns down in front of them.

"Now, turn around real slow. Keep your hands where I can see them." The two men slowly turned around.

Jerry looked the man over. Total redneck, old guy. *He's not going to be fast enough if I do something,* he thought to himself. Then he saw some movement in the bushes. *Earl.*

"Hey, Jimmy, come on out," the redneck said. "I've got these guys under control."

"Why," came a voice from behind them, by the truck. He sounded like a scared teenager.

"You've got to make your first kill sometime," he said. "No walking away from it this time. Get over here, boy."

"No," the voice said.

"Oh, shit, you've got to be kidding me," the redneck said with an exasperated tone. "Alright. You two, get down on your knees."

Jerry and Charlie looked at each other. Jerry cracked a slight smile, and then made his eyes point over past the redneck. Charlie nodded, and they kneeled down. Then Earl's rifle went off. The redneck fell to the ground, his gun flying off to the side. Charlie dived for it, then turned and shot the younger man dead. Jerry looked at him with disbelief.

"Why'd you do that?" he asked. "That was just a kid, and he was afraid to kill us."

"Use your head, Jerry," Charlie said. "We don't have a place to keep prisoners, and this kid was going to try to get back to his group. No way am I letting him leave."

Jerry just shook his head.

"We're at war, Jerry. Think about it."

Earl came walking over, rubbing his shoulder where the rifle butt was.

"Damn, forgot how hard this damn thing kicks," he said.

"Nice shot," Jerry said.

"I had to wait until you guys were down," Earl said. "This 30-06 might have gone through this creep and hit you. I was afraid he was going to shoot you as you stood."

"I saw you in the bushes," Jerry said. "I was trying to figure out a way to hit the dirt and not have that old coot shoot either of us."

"Charlie shot the kid?" Earl asked.

"Yep," Charlie said. "Jerry is a little mad about that." Earl looked over at Jerry.

"We're at war with these folks, Jerry. C'mon. I would've shot him too."

"He's not as young as you're thinking, either. This kid is in his twenties… look at him," Charlie said, standing over the body.

"Ok, I get it, guys," Jerry said.

"I'll knife the tires," Charlie said.

"Wait!" Jerry said. "Let's take a look first. We might want to drive this thing into the park. We might be able to use it."

"Good point. Let's see what's inside," Earl said.

"You recognize this truck, Earl?" asked Jerry.

"Naw, they probably stole it from somebody."

"That SUV is still here too…..actually we ought to look for more tread tracks back here. How do we know this is the only vehicle?"

"Yeah, Jerry, I was thinking the same thing," Charlie said. "Let's take a real careful look."

The three men moved around the parking lot looking for any tracks that looked fresh. They didn't see anything other than the tracks from the pickup truck.

Alright, let's see what's inside these," Jerry said. He opened the door of the SUV.

"Are the keys in the SUV?" asked Charlie.

"No," Jerry said.

"The keys are in the pickup, so we can just drive it back. We'll need to disable that one."

"Knife the tires?" Jerry asked.

"No, I wouldn't do that. Let's yank the coil wire or something like that. Something we can fix."

"Gotcha," Jerry said. "Whoa, there's a bunch of supplies in the back of this SUV."

"Really," Earl said. "What?"

"Canned food, guns and ammo, beer, bottled water, and smokes," Jerry said. "Shoot, I wish we had keys for this thing, so we could drive it to the park too."

"Heads up!" shouted Jackson as he walked out of the woods towards them.

"Everything cleaned up back there?" asked Charlie.

"Yeah, looks like," he said. "The Sheriff is keeping watch while Frank is walking around with the dog looking for anybody who might be hiding. And by the way, I know why those folks were here, I think."

"Why is that?" asked Charlie.

"They were picking up their dead. They have six bodies piled up right over there," he said, pointing over to the right. "There's a pile of guns, ammo, and other stuff next to them."

"Check for car keys to this SUV," Jerry said.

"Will do," Jackson said. "May have to go through some pockets....one of the guys we shot today might have them."

"So they were going to cart off their dead," Charlie said. "We ought to finish that job. Load the dead guys into the back of the truck and dump them somewhere. If we don't, it's going to start smelling real bad back here."

"Good point," Jerry said.

"I'll back the truck over by them," Charlie said. He got in and fired it up, then moved it over to where Jackson pointed. He got out and helped Jackson load the bodies into the truck bed. Earl came over and helped. They had all six bodies in the truck, and then they started going through the pile of stuff. There were six handguns, and five long guns with ammo. No keys for the SUV.

"We still need to pick up the other six bodies, but we might want to dump these ones first," Jackson said. "It's going to be hard to lift the other bodies on top of these."

"I'll call Hilda and ask her if there's a canyon nearby that we can dump them," Charlie said. He pulled out his cellphone and dialed her number.

"Hilda?"

"Yes, Charlie. What's been going on back there?"

"We killed another six bad guys. We've got twelve bodies to get rid of now. Is there a canyon close by that we can dump them in? They are going to stink pretty soon."

"Yes, get on that road back there, but go south instead of north. There are some switchbacks there as the road climbs into the hills. You can dump the bodies off of the cliff next to the big turnout."

"Alright. Is that the way to get back to the front of the RV Park?"

Bug Out! Part 3 – Motorhome Madness

"Yes, basically. There's a spur off of that road, right before it widens into two lanes on each side. It goes off to the right. That will bring you into the side entrance to the front parking lot."

"Alright, then we'll dump the bodies there. I'll call you before we head back. We are going to bring the pickup truck to the park, and the SUV too if we can find the keys. It's full of supplies."

"Alright. Be careful. I take it nobody got wounded this time."

"Nope, everybody is fine. Talk to you soon." Charlie put the phone back in his pocket.

"Hey, found the SUV keys," Jerry said. "The redneck that was going to shoot us had them in his pocket."

"Excellent," Charlie said. "Hilda told me where to go to dump the bodies. Who wants to go with me? I'm going to take the first load."

"I'll go," Earl said.

"Me too," Jackson said.

"Alright, I'll go check out the bodies of the other guys. May need help dragging them, though."

"We can probably get the truck back in there if we're careful," Charlie said has he got behind the wheel. Earl and Jackson got into the cab next to him, and he drove out onto the road.

Jerry took the keys and got into the SUV. He cranked it, and the engine fired up.

"Excellent," he said to himself. He shut it back off, and then got out. Frank came walking up with Lucy by his side.

"It's clear back there, and the Sheriff is keeping watch up in the blind. What's going on here?"

"Body disposal, mainly," Jerry said. "There were six from the first fire fight. We think this second group of guys were here to pick up bodies, but I think they were also coming back to get this SUV. It's full of supplies."

"Really," Frank said. "So I take it Charlie took off with Earl and Jackson to get rid of the first load?"

{ 67 }

"Yep. Want to help me go through the bodies of the new guys?"

"Sure. Might be something worth keeping."

"Yeah, not a lot of stuff on them, but the old guy there had the keys to the SUV in his pocket."

"That other one looks kind of young," Frank said, looking at the body laying over to the left.

"Yeah, I was a little pissed at Charlie for shooting him, but he convinced me that it was a good idea."

"So the kid didn't have a gun pointed at you guys?"

"Oh, he did, but the old guy wanted him to kill Charlie and me. The kid didn't want to, so the old guy had us get down on our knees. Earl nailed him at that point, but then Charlie grabbed his gun and shot the kid."

"Why?"

"He said we aren't set up to handle a prisoner, and we can't trust him to be free around here."

"You know, that does make a little sense," Frank said. "I probably would have just tied his hands and held him for the Major, but then we don't know if the Major is coming back here. I'm a little worried, because it's been a while."

"I know, that's what got me cooled down about it. Charlie's a careful guy. Can't blame him for that. Anyway, let's go check out the bodies back in the woods. Should be four of them by my count. Maybe we can drag them to a place that the pickup can get close to."

"Alright," Frank said. "I'd take the keys out of that SUV just in case."

"Good idea," Jerry said. He walked over to it, opened the door, grabbed the keys, and locked it.

"We need to shout out to the Sheriff when we get back there," Frank said. "So we don't get blasted with that scattergun."

Jerry nodded. They got back into the woods and over the creek.

"Sheriff, heads up," Frank shouted. "Jerry and I are coming back."

"Where are the rest of the guys?" he shouted back.

"Body disposal duty," Jerry yelled.

"Oh," the Sheriff said. "Not a bad idea, it's going to get smelly back here."

Frank and Jerry went to all four of the bodies, and picked up their guns, also emptied their pockets. Along with the weapons, they found ammo, rations, and assorted other stuff. They put it all in the knapsack that one of the Jihadists was wearing, and carried it back to the parking area, arriving there just as Charlie drove the truck back in.

"Stripped those other bodies, huh?" Earl said, looking at the knapsack as he got out of the passenger side door.

"Yeah," Jerry said. He unlocked the back of the SUV and dumped it in. "Let's go get those other bodies."

Jackson got out of the cab, and then Charlie. Everybody but Charlie went back to carry bodies up. They got them piled up in front of the truck, and hoisted them in. Then Charlie, Earl, and Jackson got back in the truck again, and took off.

"Well, there's a good job done," Frank said. Jerry looked at him and nodded.

"We have to get that schedule started for the blind back here," he said.

"I know, and we need to make sure we have reliable people back there."

"I wouldn't be too hard on the kid, Frank. He wasn't cut out for this kind of stuff."

"I know. We're probably lucky that things happened like they did."

"I'm surprised you handle yourself so well."

"So am I," Frank said. "I've always been a good shot, but I never killed anybody before."

"Well, back to the blinds. I'm thinking we ought to always have two people up there, not just one."

"Yeah, Jerry, I agree. Would have helped in both of our battles."

"What are your thoughts about sticking around?"

"We need to find out what happened to the Major and his guys," Frank said. "If they got killed back there, then I think we might want to get the heck out of here. I think it would take a pretty good force to take the Major out. Probably more of a force than we can handle."

"After we get this job done, maybe we ought to take a vehicle and go up north looking for them."

"Think so?"

"Maybe," Jerry said. "Let's discuss it with the group when we get back."

"Look, here comes Charlie," Frank said, pointing. The truck pulled over next to them, and Charlie motioned them over.

"One of you guys want to follow me in that SUV? Hilda told me how to get back to the front gate."

"I'll walk back through the forest and let the Sheriff know what's going on," Frank said. "I need to grab Lucy's leash on the way through anyway."

"Alright, I'll drive the SUV, then," Jerry said. "Let's go." He jumped into the SUV and fired it up. He waited for the truck to get to the driveway, and then he backed out and drove after them. Frank went back into the woods, Lucy bouncing along just in front of him with her tail wagging.

"Sheriff, I'm going back into the park," Frank shouted.

"Alright," the Sheriff shouted back. "I'll stay out here for a little while."

"You need a rifle?"

"Naw, the Deputy has my rifle up here," he replied.

"OK, see you in a little while," Frank said. He headed to the back gate, looking around carefully as he walked. He got to it, went through, and pulled Lucy's leash off the fence. He bent down to put it on her, and then walked back to the front of the park. He arrived right as the truck and SUV were pulling through the gate. Hilda was down there to meet them.

"Wow, that's a lot of stuff," Hilda said, looking in the SUV.

"Yep, worth bringing in, that's for sure," Charlie said.

"You got rid of all the bodies?"

"Yes, they're gone. Heard anything from the Major?"

"Not a peep," Hilda said. She got a concerned look on her face.

"Where do you want us to park these?"

Hilda thought about it for a moment.

"Put them back behind the clubhouse, in front of the maintenance building," she said. "That isn't visible from outside of the park."

"Alright, be back in a minute. Jerry, follow me."

They drove the vehicles behind the clubhouse. Frank went into the store, followed by Hilda, and they went up the back steps to the roof. Jeb and Jane were sitting up there.

"Sounds like I missed some fireworks," Jeb said, grinning.

"Yep, that was as hairy as the first battle," Frank said.

"I'd say worse," Jerry said as he walked up onto the roof. "An old redneck got the drop on Charlie and me. If Earl wouldn't have taken him out, we might not be alive right now."

"Now don't go getting Hilda upset," Charlie said as he got on the roof to join them.

"Too late," Hilda said. "What happened back there? Don't sugar coat it."

"Well, the Deputy lost his nerve when these cretins showed up," Frank said. "When we got back there, one of the Islamists was on his way up the ladder to get into the blind."

"Yeah, until you blasted him," Jerry said. Jane walked over to Frank and gave him a hug. She was trembling.

"I'm OK, sweetie," Frank said, looking down at her and petting her head. "Anyway, we shot the guy on the ladder, and then some other guys opened fire on us. We shot three more guys in the forest during that fire fight. Then Charlie and Jerry snuck over to the parking area to disable the vehicle so survivors would be able to get away. That's where the redneck got the drop on them. He had them covered, and was about to shoot them when Earl blasted him with his 30-06. There was another guy with him, and Charlie grabbed the redneck's gun and shot him with it. That's pretty much it."

"The rest of the time we spent getting the bodies from both of those fights out of there," Jerry said, "and taking their truck and SUV. The SUV is chock full of supplies. That's probably the main reason they came back, although they had also picked up the bodies of the first six and moved them over next to the pickup truck."

"So we've taken out twelve of these guys now," Jeb said. "They're gonna be pissed, and they know where we are. We'd better get ready."

Earl and Jackson came up onto the roof.

"What's going on?" Earl asked.

"I just told these folks what happened back there," Frank said. "Have a seat."

"So how are we going to protect ourselves against these dudes?" Jackson asked as he and Earl sat. "We've been pretty damn lucky so far."

"I agree, we've been real lucky," Jerry said. "Frank and I were talking back there. We think it would be a good idea to have the blind manned with two people instead of just one."

"Why?" asked Jeb.

"It will be harder for anybody to get the drop on us that way," Frank said.

"Alright, that makes sense," Jeb said. "Do we have enough qualified folks to do that?"

"Probably," Charlie said. "I wouldn't put two of our top people in there at a time, though. One top person and a second person that isn't quite so experienced ought to do it."

"For the next 24 hours, I'd make it two top people," Jerry said. "I agree with Charlie after that. If we are going to get hit again, I suspect it will be sooner rather than later."

"Hey, look," Jeb said. "Here comes the Humvee. The Major is driving."

{ 7 }

Ambush!

The Humvee drove up to the front of the park. Hilda ran down the stairs and over to the gate to meet them and let them in. She looked inside. It was just the Major, one of the privates, and somebody laying down in the back.

"Hi," the Major said. "Hilda, right?"

"Yes, Major. Do you have wounded?"

"My Lieutenant. Is there a doctor nearby?"

"Yes, I can get one here in just a few minutes. I'll go call him. You can pull over by the clubhouse. We have a stretcher in there."

"Thanks so much," he said, and he drove forward and parked. He got out as Frank, Jerry, and Charlie came running over.

"You alright, Major Hobbs?" asked Frank.

"No, I'm not alright. We took a real beating back there," he said.

"How badly is the Lieutenant wounded?"

"Looks like he'll recover, but he's lost a fair amount of blood. I'll need to get an airlift set up to get him out of here. Is there a field large enough here to put down a chopper?"

"You're best bet is probably that front parking lot," Hilda said as she walked back over. "Doc is on his way, and he'll bring the ambulance and paramedics too, just in case. Anybody else need medical attention?"

The Major shook his head no, and so did the private, who was getting out of the passenger seat.

"What happened?" Jerry asked.

"I'll tell you in a few minutes, after the doctor gets here. Did you guys see any more action? We thought we heard gunfire coming from this direction."

"Yes, six more fighters came to the back," Charlie said. "They were attempting to pick up that SUV and get the bodies of their dead. We killed all of them."

"Good," he said. "Look like the same folks?"

"Yep, a mixture of Islamist fighters and militia men," Frank said.

Earl and Jackson walked over, with Jane and Lucy.

"What's up?" asked Earl. Jane went over next to Frank.

"The Lieutenant is wounded," Hilda said. "The doc is on his way over here."

Just then the doctor's car pulled in through the front gate, followed by the paramedic's vehicle. Hilda went over to greet them, and pointed to the Humvee. They drove over there. The paramedics jumped out of their vehicle, and brought out a gurney. The doctor got out of his car and rushed over.

"Who's injured?" he asked.

"Lieutenant James," the Major said. "He's in the back of the Humvee."

The doctor nodded at the two paramedics, and they brought the gurney around behind the Humvee. The Private opened the doors, and the paramedics carefully put the Lieutenant on it.

"Take him inside the clubhouse and I'll have a look," the doctor said.

The paramedics pushed the gurney inside, and the doctor followed it. Jasmine and Rosie were still in the clubhouse, with Chester and a couple other people.

Bug Out! Part 3 – Motorhome Madness

"Turn some more lights on in here, would you, Hilda?" the doctor said.

"Sure thing." She hit the switch and the lights came on.

"What wrong with him?" asked Rosie.

"Shoulder wound," the doctor said after he pulled back the bloody shirt. "Not life threatening, but he's lost some blood. We'll need to get him to a hospital. How long has he been unconscious?"

"Not that long," the Major said. "Probably about half an hour."

"Alright. We have a small hospital in town….the boys could have him there in about ten minutes."

"Great," the Major said. "I figured we'd need to do an airlift. Go ahead and take him there."

The doctor nodded to the paramedics, and they rolled the gurney out to their vehicle and loaded him in. Then they took off.

The major wrote a phone number on a piece of paper and handed it to the doctor.

"Here's my number, give me a call and let me know how he is after you've patched him up."

"Will do," the doctor said, and then he rushed back out to his car and jumped in. He followed the paramedic's vehicle down the road to town. Hilda went out and got the gate closed up again. Then she came back into the clubhouse.

"You two hungry?" asked Hilda.

"Yes," the Major said. The private nodded yes too.

"Alright, let me whip something up for you," she said, as she walked towards the clubhouse kitchen.

"What's been happening here?" asked the Major.

"Remember the murder we were investigating?" asked Frank.

"Yes, the old man with the short wave radio," he said.

"We figured out who did that. It was the woman that was in his rig with him the night before. Cynthia."

"Really? How did you figure that out?"

{ 77 }

"She disappeared, and on the way out she broke into Jerry's rig and stole that short wave radio," Frank said. "Then we found out that she was the lover of the militia leader.

"Which militia leader?"

"Franklin J. Hornady," Earl said.

"Franklin?" asked Chester. He laughed.

"Oh, that guy," the Major said. "He's been in custody for a couple days now. He lost control of the Williams Militia, and the new leader tried to kill him. He surrendered to us for his own protection."

"No, really?" asked Jackson.

"Really," the Major said. "He's quite a blowhard, that guy."

"I don't think Franklin ever had control of that Militia in the first place," Chester said.

"Who's the leader now?" asked Jerry.

"We aren't sure," the Major said. "I don't think the Williams Militia is the core of this group, though. It's too big and sophisticated now, and they have an alliance with the Islamists. The little Williams Militia never could have put that together themselves. Very strange. We don't know where these other folks are coming from."

"So you aren't sure who's the leader is, but it sounds like you have an idea," Jerry said. "Who do you think?"

"If I were a betting man, I'd say that weirdo they call Officer Simmons, and one of the Islamist leaders."

Jane looked like she was going to faint. Frank steadied her. Jasmine came over and leaned against Jerry.

"You guys know who that is, I take it. Maybe we talked about him when I was here before?" asked the Major.

"Yeah, Frank here shot him on the way out of Williams," Chester said.

"Maybe you told me about that, too," the Major said. "Sorry, I'm still a little rattled."

"What happened to you guys up the road?" asked Frank.

Bug Out! Part 3 – Motorhome Madness

The Major looked down and collected his thoughts.

"We took off on that road heading north. It was almost completely deserted out there. We passed a couple of ranches, but that was about it. Real rugged terrain on both sides of the road. Then we see a Honda CRV off to the side of the road, with its hood open."

"Uh Oh," Charlie said. "What color?"

"Red," he said. "Why?"

"Sounds like Cynthia's car."

"Oh no," Hilda said.

"Anyway, I asked my men to get out to see if we could render any assistance. I stayed in the Humvee, trying to get the command post on the radio. The Lieutenant and the privates all got out and walked over. There was nobody around the car. Then we started taking small arms fire from the ridges. I looked around, and realized that we had driven right into a perfect spot for an ambush. Narrow road, with high ridges on either side. No place to hide."

"Crap," Jerry said.

"Three of the privates got killed right away. The Lieutenant jumped for cover, but got hit in the shoulder. Private Jones here got over to him, and we all started to return fire."

"The Lieutenant was still in action then?" asked Frank.

"Yes. He didn't seem that badly wounded at that point. We were able to nail two guys on the right ridge and one on the left. Then a person on the right ridge stood up and got ready to throw a grenade. The Private shot him before he could throw it, and it went off in his hand. He must have had others on his person or close by, because we heard a few others go off."

"So they did have the grenades," Jerry said. "We were wondering if those were from you or them."

"Oh, we have some, but it's hard to throw them up a cliff."

"Where are the bodies of the three privates?" asked Charlie.

{ 79 }

"Back on the road. We pulled them over to the side. We were getting ready to load them in the Humvee when the Lieutenant passed out. We loaded him in the back and hi-tailed it here."

"Do you think you got all of the enemy back there?" asked Frank.

"No way to tell. Private Jones climbed up on the right ridge. It was a mess after the grenade went off. Everybody up there was dead, but there was no way to tell if others escaped."

"You didn't get up to the left ridge?"

"No, we were going to do that next, but then the Lieutenant passed out."

"You say that you don't think the Williams Militia is a big part of this group now?" asked Earl.

"That's what we are hearing. In fact, that's what Franklin J. Hornady told us. I tend to believe him on that, but not much else."

"I was in that group, Major," Earl said. "It's bothered me that I didn't recognize any of the militia men we killed. We've nailed seven of them so far, back by the blinds. I got a good look at all of the bodies, because we loaded them up into a pickup this morning and dumped them down a canyon. I didn't know any of them, I'm sure of that. Didn't recognize the vehicles either."

"I was wondering why you didn't mention that you recognized anybody," Jerry said.

"Why did you dump the bodies?" asked the Major.

"They were going to stink up the back end of the park," Charlie said.

"Oh," said the Major. "Stupid question. Sorry. I assume you stripped the bodies of whatever they were carrying."

"Of course," Charlie said. "Remember that SUV back there?"

"Yeah," the Major said.

"It was full of supplies in the back. We have it over behind the clubhouse if you want to take a look."

"Later," Hilda said, as she carried out two plates of food. She put one in front of the Major and one in front of the Private. "Want a beer with these?"

"Water would be better," the Major said. "We need to keep a clear head. We weren't that far back on the road when we were ambushed. I'd say no more than five miles. There are bad guys around here. We need to be sharp."

"Any chance of getting more troops out here?" asked Charlie.

"Oh, yeah, we'll get more out here to clean up this area," the Major said. "My CO was reluctant when we thought it was just a two-bit local militia. Now that the Islamic fighters are involved too, they will focus on this area big time."

"Good," Charlie said.

"Do you think we should be staying here, Major?" asked Jane.

"Yes, at least until we find out where the bad guys are," he said. "I'd hate to see you guys get hit out on the road like we did. A grenade on a motor home would cause one heck of a fireball. They would hit the first one in the caravan, which would block up the road, and then they would kill off all the rest that are stuck behind. Makes me shudder just thinking about it."

Jane had a horrified look on her face as she processed that information.

"So we need to get the Army in here to take these bad guys out, and we need to fortify this park as much as we can," Jane said.

"Yes, that's pretty much where we're at," the Major said. He was just finishing the meal. "Thanks, Hilda. That was great. I'm going out to the Humvee to get my CO on the radio. Be back in a few minutes." He got up to leave, and the private followed him out.

"Wow," Jasmine said. "This is really getting scary."

"You're telling me," Hilda said. She looked around the room. Everybody seemed to be deep in thought.

{ 81 }

"Maybe I should go out to the site of the ambush and look around," Jerry said.

"Why?" asked Jasmine. She didn't look happy.

"Because I'm an expert tracker, and I'll be able to tell if anybody escaped, more than likely."

"That's not a bad idea, actually," Charlie said. "I could go too…..I'm not a bad tracker myself. Too bad Jeb is laid up, because he's the best tracker I've ever seen."

The Major walked back in with a smile on his face.

"Well, I got their attention. The CO is sending a platoon out here."

"How many in platoon?" asked Rosie.

"About 36, plus equipment," Jerry said. "That's about right for this job, at least to find the enemy."

"Yep," the Major said.

"If you'd like, I'll go out to the site of the ambush and check for tracks," Jerry said. "I'm an expert tracker."

"Appreciate it, but let's wait until the men get here. That info isn't important to us at this point….we know these guys are part of a much larger force. The CO said that there have been a couple of other incidents to the north of here also."

"Oh, really," Charlie said. "How much larger are they thinking?"

"The CO said they could be as large as five hundred men, but they appear to be poorly supplied. That's probably why they keep trying to hit this place."

"So that tells me they'll make another attempt to get back here for that SUV," Jerry said. "I didn't count everything in there, but I'll make a rough guess that there's at least a few thousand rounds of ammo in there."

"Is it ammo that you can use?" asked the Major.

"Well, it is now," Jerry said. "It's 7.62, and we've got nine AK-47s now. Took them off of the bodies back there in the forest. Now I'll have something better than that M-1 Carbine to shoot, and I'm checked out on the AK."

"Alright, my suggestion is that you keep them, and get more people checked out on them," the Major said. "My CO made clear to me that the platoon will be here to hunt down the enemy, not to protect an RV Park, so you guys are going to be on your own to a degree."

"I figured that would be the case," Frank said. "But the added pressure you put on them might tend to keep them away from here."

"True enough," the Major said, "but I wouldn't let your guard down. You might want to skip Happy Hour for a while."

"Oh no!" Rosie said. Then she cracked a smile. "Just kid."

Several of the people laughed.

"Jerry, you have any experience with networking and surveillance systems?" asked Frank.

"Not as much as you do, but yes, I have some. What did you have in mind?"

"If we can get the stuff we need, maybe we can rig up a good early warning system here. Eventually somebody is going to go around those deer blinds."

"What do we need?" asked Jerry.

"Well, I suspect that we have plenty of cabling and network hubs, since this park has Wi-Fi," Frank said. "Is there a store in town that might have things like security cameras and monitors?"

Hilda started to laugh.

"That's two I owe Jer," she said. "Follow me."

She got up and headed for the back of the clubhouse. There was a door to the outside. She unlocked it and they went through. It lead to the maintenance area, where they had parked the SUV and the pickup truck.

"I fought Jer about that fence back there, and I fought him about this," she said, as she unlocked the padlock on the maintenance

{ 83 }

building door. It was a corrugated metal building that looked about fifty years old. "Who knew that we'd end up needing both?" She turned on the lights.

"Is that what I think it is?" asked Frank, looking at the boxes up on the top shelf.

"Yep, a complete security camera system," Hilda said. "Jer spent a few thousand on this. I was so mad at him. Then he got sick, and never could get it set up."

"Is this stuff still good?" asked Jerry.

"Hmmmmm. A little old school, but it will work as long as it's not damaged," Frank said. "Give me a hand, and we'll pull these boxes down onto the work bench."

Jerry got up next to him, and they picked up the first box. It was heavy, and they struggled to get it down.

"Damn, what's in this?" asked Jerry.

"I'm guessing it's a DVR unit and some network stuff."

They picked up the second box and put it down there. It was a bunch of cameras and wires, in white Styrofoam, with a cardboard and cellophane top over it. It wasn't heavy.

"Wow, thirty six cameras," Jerry said. "That ought to give us some decent coverage."

"Yes, definitely," Frank said.

"He wanted to buy monitors too, but I put a stop to it, I'm afraid," Hilda said.

"No problem," Frank said. "I'll rig this thing up so we can display any camera on any PC or iPAD in the park."

"How long will it take?" asked Hilda.

"A good couple of days," Frank said.

"I'll bet those spools of wire go with this," Jerry said, pointing to them on the shelf.

Bug Out! Part 3 – *Motorhome Madness*

"Probably," Frank said. "This is where the old school hardware hurts us a little bit. The newer systems are wireless. This is more secure, though."

"Can you guys put this up yourself, or will we need to recruit some folks?" asked Hilda.

"Jasmine knows this stuff like the back of her hand, from work," Jerry said, "so that makes three of us."

"Jane has some background too," Frank said. "Some of the most time-consuming tasks don't take knowledge, though. Like stringing wire, for instance, and installing cameras."

"Alright, let's get back to the clubhouse and see if we can get this organized," Hilda said. She waited for Frank and Jerry to walk out of the maintenance building, and then she locked it back up. "Since there may be more moles around, I think we'd better mind the security on this stuff."

"Yeah, damn straight," Jerry said. Frank nodded, and they went back into the clubhouse.

"What's up?" asked Charlie.

"I just showed them all of that security camera stuff that Jer bought a few years ago."

"You still have that? Jer told me you were pushing him to sell it."

"I was, but then he started to get sick, so it just got stored in the maintenance building."

"Security cameras?" asked the Major. "That would be a good thing to set up."

"Yep, we'll get started on it in a few minutes," Frank said.

Suddenly there was a rifle shot, coming from the front of the park.

"Jeb," Charlie said. "We've got company."

The men all rushed outside and cautiously looked at the gate. Cynthia was there, silently looking inside. Something didn't look right about her. She was in a daze.

{ 85 }

"She's got something on under that dress," the Private said. "It looks too bulky."

"Help me!" cried Cynthia. "Let me in, please."

{ 8 }

Double Agents

Cynthia stood outside the gate, in a daze, crying out to be let in.

"Look at that dress. It's not hanging right," Jane said, as she walked over to Frank.

"Major, that woman has a suicide bomber's vest on under that dress," shouted Private Jones.

"Let me in, please!" cried Cynthia. She started to lift her hands, but one of them stopped at about waist level.

"There's the detonator," Jerry said, pointing. Then there was a loud shot, and Cynthia's hand exploded, flesh and blood and black plastic and metal flying everywhere. She fell to her knees, wailing.

"Who shot?" asked Major Hobbs.

"Jeb," Frank said. "What do we do now?"

"Sometimes those vests are booby trapped… you try to take them off, and kaboom," Jerry said.

"Yes, I'm well aware of that," the Major said. He was thinking, trying to shut everything else out.

"What if we just shot her in the torso?" asked Earl. "Wouldn't that set off the explosives?"

"Probably not," the Major said. "Besides, that's murder."

"No, that's self-protection," said Jerry. "You know that she's probably responsible for the loss of your three privates, right? That red CRV was hers."

"I'm aware of that too, Jerry," Major Hobbs said, "but we are still a civilized country. We can beat these guys without being like them."

"Alright, let's problem solve, here, folks," Frank said. "Who knows anything about disarming one of those vests?"

"I had some training a few years ago, but it's not up to date," the Major said. "Private?"

"No sir, sorry," he said. "Why don't you get on the horn to the CO and ask him to send somebody with that Platoon?"

"You are continuing to impress me, Private," Major Hobbs said.

"If they don't get here fairly quickly, she's going to be in bad shape, out in the hot sun with no water," Hilda said.

"Well, I'd throw her my bottle of water, but that takes two hands to open," Jackson said. "I'm certainly not going to walk up to her. In fact, we probably aren't far enough back. They usually put ball bearings and washers on top of the explosives, and we could get hit."

"Jackson is right about that," Jerry said. "We should move over behind the building."

"On the water, I've got some of those pull top bottles in my rig," Frank said. "Those take one hand and your teeth to open. I'll go get one and toss it to her."

"I'll go with you," Jane said. "We need to feed Lucy and Mr. Wonderful anyway." They walked off together, with Lucy bouncing along in front of them.

"So what do you think?" Jane asked.

"About?"

"Staying here," Jane said. "Are we going to live through all of this?"

"I don't think we have a choice about staying here, but I don't like being this close to the front lines. Setting up a security system will help, but all it does is give us early warning. If a force of 40 or 50 shows up here with military equipment, we are going to be in trouble."

"I'm thinking the same thing," Jane said. "I don't want you back in that blind again. I want you to work the security system instead."

"I might not have a choice, but remember the new rule.....two people at a time."

"If you go up there, I'm going too," Jane said. Her voice was starting to break up.

"It's alright," Frank said, pulling her close.

"I'm sorry I used to disrespect you. And minimize you," Jane said.

"What are you talking about?"

"You know," Jane said. "I didn't have enough confidence in you, and I picked at you."

"We act like an old married couple always does, sweetie," Frank said. "I could always tell that you loved me. Getting a push from you has been helpful more times than I can count. But why all of this now?"

"I'm afraid that this is going to be over soon, and one or both of us are going to be dead," Jane said.

They stopped in front of their rig. Frank looked down at Jane, and then hugged her tightly. He could feel her sobbing. The dog sat down and looked up at them. She turned her head to the side and started crying.

"It's OK, girl," Jane said, trying to compose herself. "It's just your mom being worried."

Frank pulled away from Jane and unlocked the door of their coach. Then all three went in.

"I'll feed the girl and Mr. Wonderful," Frank said, and he got to work on that.

"Alright, I'll get the water bottle."

Frank opened the two cans of food. Mr. Wonderful sauntered over, and started to meow. He rubbed against Frank's calves.

"Sorry, sir," Frank said. "We haven't spent much time together for the past couple of days." The cat was purring loudly now.

"OK, here we go," Frank said, and he put the dishes on the floor. The two animals attacked their food quickly. Frank sat down sideways on the dinette bench and watched them.

"Well, I guess they were hungry," Jane said, walking away from the pantry with a bottle of water. She peeled the plastic seal off and pulled up on the lid to loosen it up.

"Should we let Lucy rest for a while here?" asked Frank.

"She slept for a while in the clubhouse. I think we ought to bring her. She's got better eyes and ears than we do."

"Alright, she should be done in a few minutes."

"Frank?"

"Yes?"

"Don't make plans tonight," she said. "I've got a special task for you."

Frank smiled at her.

"That sounds very interesting."

"Yes, you'll enjoy it," Jane said, her face flushing.

Lucy finished, and Frank and Jane got out of the coach with her. Frank locked up. He could hear a gentle protest from Mr. Wonderful.

"Mr. Wonderful is needing some attention too, you know," Frank said, chuckling.

"Me first."

The two held hands as they walked back over to the clubhouse.

"Here's that water bottle," Frank said. "How close can I safely get to her?"

"I'll take it, sir," the Private said. "I've got body armor on, so I have some protection." He took the bottle from Frank, and approached Cynthia.

"Cynthia!" the Private yelled. "Here's some water. I'm going to toss it to you."

She looked up at him. She was still crying, and there was a look of hatred in her eyes.

"I don't want your water, pig," she spat out between sobs. The private threw the bottle to her anyway, and it landed well within reach. He turned and quickly walked back to the group.

"Wow, nice personality," the Private said with a smirk.

"You don't know the half of it," Jackson said.

The Major walked over from the Humvee.

"There was already somebody qualified to deal with the vest in the platoon, and they are on their way here. They should be here in about twenty minutes."

"Excellent," Frank said.

"So what are we going to do with her once we have her disarmed?" asked Charlie. "We don't have a good place to lock her up."

"Private Jones and I will take her with us," the Major said.

"You're leaving?" asked Hilda.

"Yes, for a little while," he said. "The CO wants to interview both of us. We'll probably be back here after that. We need to collect the Lieutenant, for one thing."

"She's too defiant for the Militia now," Jerry said, looking over at Cynthia. "I'll bet she's gotten close to somebody on the Islamist side. She might even have been the facilitator in getting them together."

"I doubt that," the Major said. "They don't put valuable people in suicide vests."

"Well, I guess that's a good point," Jerry said. "I'll grant you that."

"Hey, Jerry, want to help me start planning the security system?" asked Frank.

"Sure, might as well get started," Jerry said. They walked into the clubhouse, followed by Jane and Lucy, Hilda, and Earl. The rest of the folks stayed outside and kept an eye on Cynthia.

"Hilda, do you have any big sheets of paper?"

"I do, and some easels too," she said. "Jer bought some of that stuff when he was trying to get us into the Corporate Retreat market. Never worked. Jer was full of ideas like that."

"Wish I would have met him," Frank said.

"He would have liked you," Hilda said. She turned and went into the back room of the clubhouse, and returned with the easel and two pads of large paper. "This do?"

"Perfect," Frank said.

"Oh, yeah, and these," she said. She pulled several felt tip markers out of her pocket.

Jerry grabbed the easel and set it up. Frank picked up one of the pads of paper and hung it on with the two bolts at the top, and then picked up one of the markers.

"Hilda, could you give me one of the maps of the park? Mine is back in my rig."

"Sure thing, just a sec," she said. She walked back into the storage room again, and came out with a map. Frank looked at it, and then drew a rough version of it on the large paper. He put in landmarks, and the approximate position of trees along the back.

"OK, we have 36 cameras. We need to decide where to place them."

"We have a few sensitive parts of the park that should be covered," Jerry said. "The rest ought to be pointing outward."

"Yes," Frank said. "Important places within the park. Generator room. Well and Pump area. Incoming electrical and city water supplies. Maintenance area. Anything else that you two can think of?" He looked at Hilda and Jerry.

"Internet cable hookup," Hilda said. She pointed to where it was on the map.

"Anything else?" Frank asked.

"Not that I can think of," Jerry said. Hilda nodded in agreement.

"Alright, so that is 6, and we have 30 left.

"I'd say we should put one in a tree pointing at the parking area in the back, and one pointing to the blind in such a way that you can see the blind itself and the area in front of the blind," Jerry said.

"Hopefully we have enough wire to get that far," Frank said. "I'm sure we can get to the blind, but the parking area is a ways back there."

"Maybe we can find a vantage point that can cover the parking area but isn't all the way over there."

Frank nodded.

"Wonder how far back the Wi-Fi reaches?" asked Jerry.

"I know it will reach the blind, because I was able to connect my phone to Wi-Fi when I was up there."

"Excellent," Jerry said. "That way whoever is manning the blind can pull that view up on their phone or their tablet."

"Yeah, that would make a big difference. That leaves us with 28 to place around the perimeter. Any reason not to just put them up every so many feet?"

"Not that I can think of," Hilda said.

Charlie walked in and took a look at the map on the pad of paper.

"Looks good, gentlemen," he said. "How can I help?"

"How'd you like to lead the team that strings the cable and installs the cameras?"

"It would be my pleasure," Charlie said.

"Excellent," Frank said. "Let's get this map blocked out, then we can take a picture of it on a couple of tablets and go walk the areas to take a look."

"Alright," Jerry said. "Good plan."

As they got to work on that, Earl walked back outside. He went up to Jackson.

"Anything happening?" he asked.

"Nope," Jackson said. "How are things going in there?"

"Pretty good. I think Frank really knows his stuff with networks and surveillance systems. Charlie just got put in charge of stringing cable and putting up cameras. We're liable to be asked to join that team."

"I'd be fine with that," Jackson said. "Do you think these folks trust us yet?"

"Some of 'em do. Should we have been more open with them? I think Jerry is pretty suspicious about us because we didn't say anything about Cynthia."

"No doubt. But what are we going to do? They'd never believe our story now, even though it's true. You know Cynthia will say some things about us under interrogation."

"Yes, it might be in our interest to make sure she gets a little bit dead," Earl said.

"What if we make a preemptive strike and come clean to Frank, Charlie, and Jerry?"

"I'll do it if you will, but remember that one thing. Remember why we didn't want to do that before."

"Yeah, I know," Jackson said. "I'm OK with it. Call me naïve, but these are good people. If we can help them that way, I'll do it."

"Alright, I'll go along too."

"Look, here comes the platoon!" Jackson said. They walked over closer to the main group.

There was a line of Humvees coming onto the driveway. They pulled up in the front parking lot, as far away from Cynthia as they could get. Cynthia turned around and looked at them, then turned back to the group.

"Cowards'," she cried.

The radio in the Humvee came on. Major Hobbs ran over and answered it.

"Major Hobbs here."

Bug Out! Part 3 – Motorhome Madness

"Hello, sir, this is Major Darcy. We have our vest expert ready to go. I'm assuming the subject is the woman by the front gate."

"Correct."

"Alright. The expert and two of my men will be wearing protection. I suggest that you take all of your people and your vehicle back, behind a building if possible."

"Roger that. Proceed."

He put the microphone back, and looked towards the group.

"Let's move it back here, folks," he said. "Let's get behind the store. I'm moving the Humvee back there as well."

The group followed instructions, and got back behind the store. Hilda went into the store and back to the stairs.

"Jeb, come down here," she shouted.

"Why?"

"We want you further away from Cynthia. The army is about to attempt to disarm the vest."

"Be right down," he said.

"Good, hurry," she said.

He hobbled down the stairs, carrying his .270. They joined the others outside.

Three men with bomb protection armor and helmets with large face shields walked up to Cynthia. Two of the men grabbed her arms, as she squirmed and cried from her wounded hand. The third man ripped the top of her dress down to reveal the vest. He looked at the front and the back, and then gave a thumbs up to Major Darcy, who was sitting in the lead Humvee. He undid the straps and carefully pulled the vest off. He set it about ten yards away from the two men who were holding Cynthia, and then trotted over to one of the Humvees. He picked up a folding metal box and carried it over. He put the vest into the box, and then reached in and attached a couple of wires. He took the box to the far end of the parking lot, unreeling the wire as he walked away. When he was about 50 yards away, he

{ 95 }

stopped and squatted. He pulled a device out of his pocket and hooked the wires to that. Then he twisted the knob on the top. There was a loud explosion, and the box flew about fifteen feet in the air and came back down. The bomb tech took off his helmet and walked over to where the other two men were holding Cynthia.

"We need to search her," he said. The two men continued to hold her arms as the tech patted her down. Then he made the thumbs-up sign. He pulled her dress back up as best he could, then grabbed her arms and pulled them behind her. He applied a large zip tie, and then walked her over to the lead Humvee. Major Darcy got on the radio and called Major Hobbs.

"Alright, Major Hobbs, you can open the gates now."

"Thanks, Major Darcy, will do." He put down the radio mic and looked over at Hilda. He pointed to the gate. She nodded, and went over to open it. Then the Humvees started to drive through, and they all parked up and down the road in front of the clubhouse.

"Great to see you, Darcy," Major Hobbs said, extending his hand in greeting.

"Likewise, Hobbs. Things have been a little hairy around here, from what I've heard."

"Yes. Let's go into the clubhouse and I'll brief you on what I know so far. Then I'll take off with the prisoner. The General wants to talk to me."

Outside, the group was milling around, talking.

"That was a powerful explosion," Jeb said to Frank as he walked up.

"Sure was," Frank said. "Nice job on taking out that detonator."

"Thanks. What's going to happen now?"

"Major Hobbs has to go to headquarters to brief the CO. He's taking Cynthia with him."

"I take it all these troops are here to hunt down the bad guys?"

"Yep," Frank said. "They weren't that interested until they heard that there were Islamists with the militia up here."

"What ever happened to the Sheriff?" asked Jeb.

Frank got a sick look on his face.

"Forgot he was back there with the deputy. Hope everything is alright back there....you know he heard the rifle shot and the explosion. Why hasn't he called?" Frank pulled out his phone and dialed.

"Sheriff?"

"Yes, Frank. What the hell is going on up there?"

"Cynthia came up to the gate. She had a suicide bomber vest on. It was under her dress, but we could see it. She raised her hands, getting ready to push the button on the detonator when Jeb shot it."

"So that was the rifle shot. I take it the vest got detonated?"

"Yes, the bomb tech in the platoon put it into one of those blast containers and blew it up."

"Platoon, huh? They're finally listening to us, I take it. Anything else I need to know?"

"Well, yeah, quite a bit, but maybe it better wait until you two get back down here."

"Is there anybody else available to take over back here? If not, we can hang out for a while. I've had a good time talking with my nephew."

"Not really. It's been a little crazy here. Not sure who we could send at the moment."

"Alright, then I'll just hang tight for a while, Frank. Not a problem."

"Good, talk to you later."

"He alright?" asked Jeb.

"Yeah, he's bonding with his nephew." Frank smiled.

Earl and Jackson walked up to the two men.

"Frank, we need to talk to you two and Charlie and Jerry. Can we go off somewhere for a few minutes?"

"Sure," Frank said. He made eye contact with Charlie and Jerry and motioned them over.

"What's up?" asked Jerry.

"Earl and Jackson want to talk to us about something."

"Alright, let's go over to the maintenance yard," Charlie said. "It ought to be a little quieter there. This place is a zoo all of a sudden, and the Majors are in the clubhouse."

The men walked back to the maintenance yard silently.

"Alright, what's on your mind?" asked Frank.

Earl looked at Jackson. He nodded.

"We need to come clean on some stuff," Earl said.

"Go on," Jerry said. He looked at them warily.

"We were sent into this group by the militia, to spy on you guys," Earl said. Jackson nodded.

{ 9 }

Terror from the North

The group stared at Earl and Jackson, not sure what to do next.

"You were sent in here to spy on us by the Williams Militia?" asked Charlie.

"Yes, actually by Hank," Earl said. "He knew some of you were going to make a run for it."

"You didn't help him during the end, and you fought against the militia earlier today," Charlie said. "Kinda seems like you aren't with them anymore."

"Why are you coming clean now?" asked Jerry, who was looking at them intensely.

"Cynthia knows us," Jackson said. "She'll tell under interrogation, I suspect."

"So you are only telling us because you think you are about to get caught?" asked Frank.

"Settle down, guys," Jeb said. "Let's be calm about this. I've got a real good BS detector, and I'm not sensing it with these guys."

"Why didn't you tell us about this before?" asked Jerry.

"We were afraid that you'd want us to be double agents," Earl said.

"Double agents?" asked Frank.

"They thought we would have sent them back into the Williams Militia to gather info on them, and give them phony info on us," Charlie said.

"We still might," Jerry said.

"We'll do that now, if that's what you guys want," Earl said. "You folks are good people."

"Did you ever actually start acting as a spy?" asked Jerry.

"Meaning did we ever pass any information over to the militia?" asked Jackson.

"Yes."

"No, we didn't," he replied. "We never planned on doing it, either. We wanted to get away from that group. We were just going to leave with you guys. Hank and Lewis cornered us when we were getting ready to go. If we wouldn't have agreed, they would have killed us right there."

"But you chose not to say anything later, even when you saw Cynthia?" asked Jerry.

"I know it looks bad," Earl said. "Frankly, neither of us wanted to fight for anybody. We weren't willing to risk our lives for that stupid militia, and we didn't know you guys at first, so we didn't want to risk our lives for you guys, either."

"Kinda makes you sound like sunshine patriots," Jerry said.

"Jerry, put yourself in their shoes for a minute," Jeb said. "You know I ain't no pushover. If I thought these guys were anything but friends and assets to the group, I'd be the first to pull the trigger on them."

"Assets to the group?" asked Jerry.

"Are you forgetting that Earl saved both of us today at the parking area?" asked Charlie. "He didn't have to do that."

"Alright," Jerry said. "That was a concrete action, and I am more than grateful for that."

"Damn straight," Charlie said. "You guys are alright as far as I'm concerned, regardless of how you ended up here. None of us planned to be in this situation."

"So what do we do now?" Frank asked. "Do we discuss this with the Major?"

"I wouldn't," Charlie said. "I'd say let's go on about our business. I could use these two guys on my camera installation team. You guys willing?"

"We were going to volunteer for that," Jackson said. Earl nodded in agreement.

"Alright, then let's get to work," Charlie said. "You guys can help me scope this out. Either of you guys have tablets?"

"Yeah, I've got an old iPAD. Why?" asked Earl.

"We want to take pictures of the map that Frank drew up in the clubhouse, and then walk the area with them and see what the physical details are. Where we can string cable, and where we can install the cameras."

"I gotcha," Earl said. "Good plan. Wonder how long the Majors are going to be in there talking?"

"Good question," Frank said.

"There is one job you guys can do without the drawing," Jerry said.

"What's that?" asked Charlie.

"Go find somewhere to put a camera in the back that gives a good view of the parking area, but isn't all the way back there. We are somewhat limited in the amount of cable we have."

"Yeah, we can do that now," Charlie said. "Frank, why don't you call the Sheriff and tell him we're on the way back."

"Will do," Frank said. He pulled his phone out of his pocket.

"Sheriff?"

"Yep. This Frank?"

"Yeah. Charlie, Earl, and Jackson are on the way back there. They're scouting for camera locations. Just wanted to give you a heads up."

"Camera locations?"

"Yeah, Hilda's husband bought a 36 camera security system and never put it up. We are going to use it."

"Good idea. I'll watch for them."

"Thanks, Sheriff."

Frank put his phone back in his pocket.

"Alright, Charlie, he'll be watching for you."

"Thanks, Frank," he said. "Let's go, guys."

The three men walked off. Jeb, Frank, and Jerry looked at each other.

"Well?" asked Frank.

"I don't like it, but you know how I am," Jerry said. "I've got a suspicious nature."

"And you keep that suspicious nature," Jeb said. "It's a good thing to have these days. Are you convinced that those two are OK?"

"Are you?" Jerry asked.

"Yes, I think so," Jeb said. "But we should keep our eyes open. I know Charlie will. He's more suspicious than you are. He just doesn't talk about it as openly."

"I had a feeling he was," Frank said. "Jerry and I are trying to win him back over after those arguments we had a few days ago."

"I noticed, and Charlie is trying really hard, too," Jeb said. "I have my differences with the old coot, but he's a good man. We need him with us. I would rather he not be the leader, though. He'll try to organize how you wipe your butt."

The three men cracked up.

"Yeah, I gathered that too," Frank said. He looked over at Jerry. "You OK?"

"Yes," Jerry said. "I don't like that those guys were less than truthful with us, though. I've been a little suspicious of them ever since they admitted that they knew Cynthia."

"I think Earl is still afraid we're going to use them as double agents," Frank said.

"I know," Jeb said. He looked down for a moment, thinking. "If I thought they would be useful, I'd be all for sending them in, but I'm guessing that the folks they were close to aren't even around anymore. We know Franklin isn't."

"I was thinking the same thing," Jerry said. "But it doesn't hurt to make them think we might decide to send them in."

"I'm OK with that," Frank said. "But I don't want them to worry about us accepting them as members of our group. We need men like them that are good in a fight, especially since mountain man here is a gimp now." Frank and Jerry laughed. Jeb just smiled.

"Now, be nice, guys," Jeb said. "I'm going to be better pretty quick."

"I know," Frank said. "You saved us earlier today, remember? Nice shot."

"Well, that might have been stupid," Jeb said. "It might have set off the explosive."

"Yeah, it might have," Frank said. "But it was still a good call. And now the Army has somebody they can interrogate."

"They might not get much out of her," Jerry said. "She's defiant. I've seen that behavior before, in the Gulf War."

Jane came walking over. Lucy bounded along beside her.

"What are you guys up to out here?" she asked.

"Just talking. Are the Majors done with the clubhouse yet? We need to get in there."

"Yeah, they sent me looking for you guys. Where's Charlie and the other two?"

"They're out in the back, scouting camera locations," Frank said.

"Alright, we might have to bring them back in. The Majors want to have a chat."

"I'll call them if we need to bring them in, but I'd rather not. I want those guys to get finished with the scouting," Frank said.

"Let's go back to the clubhouse," Jane said. They all walked over. Soldiers were milling around by their Humvees, and the two Majors were sitting on the veranda together.

"Where's Charlie and Earl and Jackson?" asked Major Hobbs.

"They're in the back, scouting out camera positions for our security system."

"OK, you can relay the info to them later. Come on in." The Majors went into the clubhouse, and the rest of the group followed them.

"Have a seat, folks," said Major Darcy. Everybody sat down at the long table, except Major Darcy, who stayed up to address the group. He had a grim look on his face.

"What we're about to tell you isn't top secret. I could tell the rest of your folks, but I want it to come from you guys. And I'm technically not supposed to talk about this with civilians. Things have changed, though. We are heading into some rough times, and the larger group needs to look on you folks as leaders."

"No problem," Frank said. "We don't really have a leadership, but if we have to we'll put one into place."

"Why no leadership?" asked Major Darcy.

"We didn't want a mini-government here," Frank said. "We're all private citizens. We didn't want some of us to become more 'equal' than others."

"That would be nice, if we had the luxury to go on like that," Major Hobbs said.

"What's the situation?" asked Jerry.

"You've been watching the news....so you all know that we were attacked by a wide coalition of enemies," Major Hobbs said. The people in the group nodded. He went on.

"Our country was infiltrated by agents from south of the border, mostly from south of Mexico, although there were radical Mexican Nationalist folks involved too. They engaged in low level terror attacks, looting, and general mayhem on our side of the border. At the same time, similar actions were happening on a larger scale inside Mexico, which brought their government down. Venezuela was the main source of this action, but there were other countries involved. That was step one."

"Yes, that's why we left California," Frank said. Major Hobbs nodded.

"Then we had Islamist fighters and radicals from Mexico and South America coming up over the border as a fighting force, near San Diego at first, but eventually along the entire border. That was step two."

"And I suspect the nuclear attacks were step three," Jerry said.

"Yes, that and the quick rise of radical jihad all over the Middle East, as well as in Europe. North Korea supplied the nuclear devices."

"News reports make it sound like we've got a good handle on the first three issues," Jane said.

"We wish that were the case," Major Darcy said.

"What else is going on?" Jeb asked.

"Well, you're already aware that radical militias are trying to take territory away from the United States. That's what we are seeing here, but we're also seeing it in other places."

"Is that 'step four'?" asked Jerry.

"Well, partly, but that isn't all."

"Uh Oh," Jane said.

"You have heard that there is a confederation now between the US and Mexico, and we are down there helping eradicate the radicals and Islamists, correct?"

"Yes, we've heard about that," Frank said.

"The enemy has drawn our military down there to keep them busy, as a new force of Islamist fighters starts coming over the border from Canada. It's a much larger force than we saw coming up from the southern border. We think this was always planned to be the largest part of their operation."

"Why doesn't the Canadian government do something about it?" asked Jerry.

"Canada has most of the same problems with radical Islam that the EU is having," Major Darcy said. "Infiltration into their country, even their local governments, at an alarming level. Canada is on the verge of civil war. The Canadians will win this war, we believe, but they aren't stopping the bad guys from leaving their country at this point."

"And our armed forces are spread too thin," Frank said.

"Yes, and there's a component that nobody expected," Major Hobbs said. "You know how we've been giving legal status to new immigrants if they sign up for a stint in the service?"

"Yes, of course," Jane said.

"Many of the people who took advantage of that program are enemy plants. They are firing on our troops during battles. There have been several very bad incidents."

"Oh, shit," Frank said. "So not only is the military spread thin, but the military we have is in a lot of disarray."

Major Darcy nodded.

"So what you are telling us, Major, is that the American citizens are going to have to stand up and fight," said Jeb.

"Yes, that's what I've been leading up to," Major Darcy said. "And by the way, you didn't hear the last part from me."

"I think I understand why you want us to tell the rest of the folks about this, instead of you telling them" Jeb said.

"This is horrible," Jane said. "We thought the war was almost over."

"It's going to be another civil war," Hilda said, frowning.

"Wait a minute…..don't make that comparison," Major Hobbs said. "That isn't what this is. We don't have one huge force of Americans squaring off against another huge force of Americans. We have Americans squaring off against a group of foreign enemies. Plain and simple."

"Yeah, and these idiots don't understand the American character," Frank said.

"They have no idea how many armed citizens there are in this country, either," Jeb said. "We are going to tear these creeps to shreds."

"Yes, we are, Jeb," Major Hobbs said. "And they have found that out, to a degree. We've already taken California back now due to armed private citizens. But we have to be smart. Tactics and intelligence and organization matter. We aren't fighting a bunch of un-educated gang bangers. We are fighting an organized and well supplied force of Islamist fighters, and they won't be easy on people they capture."

"We are going to have to rebuild the army," Jerry said.

"Yes," Major Hobbs said. "Major Darcy is going to find out where the Islamists are in this area. You folks are going to have to participate to take them out, and you have to do it openly. You are going to be an example to spur on others. You must become feared."

"Excuse me, but we are just a bunch of retired folks," Jane said. She was on the verge of tears.

"Speak for yourself," Jeb said. "I've been watching antics of these lowlifes for long enough. I've already taken out a few of them, and I'll make sure I take out a lot more before this is over."

"You can't even run at this point, Jeb," Hilda said.

"I can shoot, though," he said. "And I'll heal up in a week or so. Trust me."

"How much of the army can we count on?" Frank said.

"That is unclear at this point," Major Darcy said. "There are many very good immigrant men in all branches of the service. Some of them are the enemy. Most of them are good, loyal, brave Americans. We aren't finding out who the bad guys are until the heat of battle. Luckily they haven't been able to turn the tides on any major action yet."

"What about air power?" asked Jerry.

"Tough nut to crack, there," Major Hobbs said. "Washington isn't going to risk hitting Americans. We have kept the enemy forces from using air power, though. Something goes up, and we waste it pretty quick."

"They're going to get into cities and use human shields," Jane said.

Major Darcy looked at her and smiled.

"They thought they were going to do that in San Diego and LA," he said. "Doesn't work so well when the human shields shoot you."

"Yeah, New York and Chicago might need to relax their gun laws a little bit," Frank said with a grin.

"They already have," Major Darcy said.

"Do you have any more bad news, or was that it?" Jane asked.

"That was it," Major Hobbs said. "Sorry, I know this wasn't what you folks wanted to hear."

"No, it wasn't," Hilda said.

"What's next?" Frank asked.

"For us? Help you guys find the enemy nearby, and help you take them out," Major Darcy said. "Then we go on and get the next group motivated."

"There are other groups like us?" asked Jerry.

"Many."

"Good," Jerry said.

"Alright, we'll leave you folks to discuss your options. C'mon, Major Hobbs, let's go check on that intelligence. We can't spend all day here."

The two of them walked out of the Clubhouse and over to their men.

"Can this be real?" asked Jane. She was on the verge of tears.

"Oh, it's real alright," Jeb said.

"We need to get the security system up in a hurry," Frank said. Jerry looked at him and nodded.

Charlie, Earl and Jackson walked up.

"Found a perfect place to cover the parking area," Charlie said. Hilda rushed over to him and hugged him tightly. She had tears in her eyes. "What'd I miss?"

"We had a briefing with the two Majors," Frank said. "We'll let you know everything they said, and then we need to get a meeting with the larger group set up."

The three men had concerned looks on their faces.

"We need to kick this security job into high gear," Jerry said. "Let's get pictures of the map and start walking the perimeter."

"Yeah, and we'll brief these guys when we're out there," Frank said. "Hey, honey, do you have the iPAD out here?"

"Yes, it's in my purse, back by the kitchen."

Frank walked back there with her. When they got around the corner, Jane stopped.

"Can you hold me for a minute?" she asked.

Frank pulled her close and hugged her tightly as she sobbed.

"This is worse than I expected," Jane said. "This mess is going to consume the rest of our lives."

"Well, it might, but we don't know that for sure," Frank said. "We'll do what we have to do, and we'll get through it."

There was a gunshot, coming from the outside.

"Get down, everybody," Frank yelled, as he pulled Jane to the floor. He crawled up to the window and looked out. Then there were a two more shots.

He looked out the window. Major Hobbs was holding his arm, and looking down on the grass next to the roadway. Cynthia was laying there. About half of her head was gone. There was a dead soldier lying a few feet away from her.

{ 10 }

Heat of Battle

Jerry and Frank scrambled to the clubhouse windows to take a look.

"Who got shot?" Jerry asked.

"Looks like one of the soldiers took out Cynthia, and then Major Hobbs shot him," Frank replied. "Hilda, call the doc, OK?"

"Already on the phone with him, hon," Hilda said.

"Is Major Hobbs hit?" asked Jane.

"Can't tell," Frank said. He slid open the window. "Is it over, Major Hobbs?"

"Yes," he replied.

"We called the doctor," Frank shouted.

"Well, the only person who needs him is me, and it's not an emergency."

"What happened?" Frank asked.

"Oh, I just cut myself on the Humvee when I dived into shooting position," Major Hobbs said. "Stupid, but it hurts like hell."

"Can I come out?"

"Yes, don't see why not. It's over."

Frank turned to Jane.

"I'm going out there to talk with him. Be back in a minute." He pulled her head to him and kissed her forehead. "Don't worry."

"Alright. I'll keep the dog in here," Jane said.

Frank walked towards the door, and was met by Charlie and Earl and Jerry and Jackson. They walked out next to Major Hobbs and Major Darcy.

"This was one of those plants you were talking about, wasn't it?" Frank asked.

"Yes, it was," Major Darcy said. "Rodriguez. He fooled me good. I even liked the guy."

"Plants?" Charlie asked.

"Yeah," Frank said. "That was part of what we were going to tell you guys about when we were out walking the perimeter, Charlie."

"So the enemy has plants in our military?" Earl said. "Crap."

"Yes, it's not a good situation at all," Major Hobbs said.

"We were hoping to get some good info out of Cynthia," Major Darcy said. "This is a shame."

"Do you think this private knew her value?" asked Jerry.

"Could be," Major Hobbs said. "Or maybe he just guessed. We shouldn't jump to conclusions."

"No," Jerry said, "but if these plants are in easy communication with the enemy, we need to find out how. You guys just pulled in here a little while ago, so he just found out about Cynthia. If it was just a guess, that means he's willing to end his life on something that tentative. Doesn't make sense to me."

"He has a point, Major Hobbs," said Major Darcy. "We need to figure this out. We might find ourselves set up for another ambush. We might have another plant in this platoon, too. Maybe more than one."

"I take it privates aren't allowed to have cellphones," Frank said.

"Affirmative," Major Darcy said. "We don't allow that. They would have a hard time using the radio, too. It's pretty locked down unless you know what you're doing."

Bug Out! Part 3 – Motorhome Madness

"So we need to assume that they have gotten to a phone that belongs to somebody in the park," Frank said.

"Are there any pay phones around here?" asked Major Hobbs.

"Nope," Charlie said. "Pay phones are pretty much a thing of the past. I got mine torn out a couple of years ago back at my park. Everybody uses cellphones now."

"How about a private land line….in an office or something?" Frank asked.

"I'd have to ask Hilda about that," Charlie said.

A car and a paramedic vehicle pulled up to the gate. Hilda went running over to the gate and opened it. The vehicles pulled next to the store. The doctor got out and trotted over to them.

"Somebody hurt here?" he asked.

"Yeah, doc, I got a good tear on my upper arm," Major Hobbs said.

"Alright, let's get you inside so I can take a look."

The doctor and Major Hobbs walked into the clubhouse. Hilda came over and stood next to Charlie.

"Hilda, we had a question for you," Charlie said. "Do you have any land lines around the park that somebody might have used to call out?"

"Well, the payphones are all gone now," Hilda said. "I've got a land line in the office that is off of the clubhouse, and a land line in the store office, too."

"Are they locked?" asked Major Darcy.

"Yes, I keep the doors locked when I'm not in there."

"Maybe we should take a look," Charlie said. Hilda nodded.

"I'll take you to them right now."

Charlie, Hilda, Jerry, and Frank walked over to the store.

"The office is up here, by the front." She walked up there, and then stopped in her tracks. She put her hand to her mouth.

"Look, that door's been forced," Charlie said.

"Holy crap," Jerry said, looking at it.

Hilda cautiously pushed the door open. She looked over at the phone. It was sitting on the desk, but the phone wire was pulled out of the wall.

"We might have company coming here," Jerry said. "I'm going to run over to Major Darcy and tell him what happened." He sprinted out the door.

"They have to know that everybody and their brother here has a cellphone," Frank said.

"They could take out cell towers around here," Charlie said.

"I just called the doc with my cell. It wasn't a problem," Hilda said.

Frank pulled his phone out of his pocket. He took a double take.

"No service," Frank said. "Crap. We need to get men to the back and to the front of the park now. We're about to get hit." He cocked his Winchester nervously.

"Yeah, I think you're right," Charlie said. He looked over at Hilda. "Go see if the phone in the clubhouse has been taken out, and then stay there. Keep people away from the windows."

Hilda nodded, and left quickly.

"The Sheriff," Frank said. "We can't even call him on the phone at this point. We need to get people out there now."

"Yep," Charlie said. "I'll run up to the roof and give Jeb a heads up."

"Good," Frank said. "Anybody coming into the parking lot is going to get their hair parted."

Charlie nodded and smiled. "Maybe I ought to stay up there with him. My hunting rifle is still up there from earlier."

"Not a bad idea," Frank said. "I heard that you're a hell of a shot too."

Frank left the store, and ran out to where Major Darcy was. Jerry was already talking to him. Jane was out there too, with Jackson and Earl.

"Major Darcy, the cell tower is down. We're about to get hit," he shouted as he was running towards them.

"Oh no," Jane said.

"Get into the clubhouse and stay there, Jane," Frank told her. "I'll take Lucy."

"Alright," she said, and hurried into the clubhouse.

"Major, we need to put troops in the front and the back of the park. I'm worried about the Sheriff and the Deputy that are out in the blind behind the park. That's where we've been hit every other time, and I can't call him with the cell towers down."

"Roger that, Frank," the Major said. Then they both saw Major Hobbs trotting out. He had a bandage around his upper left arm, but looked good other than that.

"Somebody cut the phone line in the Clubhouse office, and my cellphone ain't connecting," Major Hobbs said. "We're about to get hit."

"So I've heard," Major Darcy said. "Frank here is suggesting putting some of our men in the back and some up here."

"Yeah, I agree," Major Hobbs said. "I've been in the back. We'll probably get hit from that direction. The front is too exposed."

"We've got two world class snipers on the roof of the store," Frank said. "We'll know pretty quickly if anything comes towards the front."

"What are they packing up there?" Major Darcy said.

"A .270 bold action and a 30-06 bolt action. Not high speed, but these guys are good out to about 400 yards, from what I've heard."

"Good," Major Darcy said. "How's the arm, Hobbs?"

"Good enough to fight," Major Hobbs said. "I'll take half the men in back....I know the terrain back there. Alright?"

"Go for it," he said. "I'll get us set up in the front."

"Let's go," Major Hobbs said. He picked out 12 men, and they headed towards the back gate, with Frank and Lucy, Jerry, Earl, and

Jackson following them. Jerry had one of the captured AK-47s and pockets full of ammo.

"You want one of these, Frank?" he asked.

"I'll stick with the Winchester for now," Frank said. "I need to stop by my coach and get the handgun and the belt and holster, though. That's where my ammo is."

"How about you two?" Jerry asked, looking at Earl and Jackson.

"I'm going to grab my hunting rifle again," Earl said. "I'll pick it up on the way."

"Same here," said Jackson. "I'd like to get checked out on the Ak-47s for next time, though."

"That reminds me," Frank said. "We need to pass along what the Majors told us when you guys were scouting for camera positions earlier."

"Maybe that ought to wait, Frank," Major Hobbs said.

"I'll give them the nutshell edition," Frank said. He looked over at the two of them. "The war is going to expand, and the army is stretched too thin. Citizens like us are going to have to take an active part in the fight, because we've got a bunch of Islamist fighters coming over the northern border."

"I knew it," Earl said. "I'm sick to death of these pajama wearing low-lifes. I'm not going down without a fight. Let's go get 'um."

"Count me in too," Jackson said.

"Good," Frank said. "We'll fill you in on the details after we get past this mess."

"If we get past this mess," Jerry said.

"Oh, we will," Major Hobbs said.

Earl and Jackson split off to go get their guns out of their coaches, and rejoined the group in a flash, before the larger group could get to the back gate. Frank got into his coach and got his handgun and his belt and holster, and ran back to the group. They filed through the gate quietly, and headed for the blind.

Bug Out! Part 3 – Motorhome Madness

"I'll sneak up close enough so I don't have to yell," Frank said. "The Sheriff knows my voice." He trotted ahead, followed by Lucy. The rest of the group kept coming at a slower rate.

"Sheriff, it's Frank," he said.

"I hear you," the Sheriff said. "What's up?"

"We're about to have company. Keep your eyes open. I have Major Hobbs and twelve of his men with me, and four of our guys."

"Wonderful," the Sheriff said sarcastically. "We'll watch for them."

The rest of the men caught up to Frank.

"We'd better not clump together like this," Major Hobbs said.

"Yeah," Jerry said. "Let's get into the same pattern we were in this morning. A group to the right, a group up the middle, and a group on the left. Let's sweep down towards the parking area. Maybe we can catch these creeps on the way in, and blow them to hell."

"I hear trucks, Frank," the Sheriff said.

"Uh Oh," Frank said. Lucy growled, but she wasn't focusing on any one area. Her nose was working. She could smell somebody coming.

"Here they come," the Sheriff said. "They're about 200 yards out, but I can hit them." They heard a bolt action rifle cock. Then a loud shot. "Got the first one. The others dived into the bushes. They think I can't see them." He laughed, and shot again.

"Nice shooting, uncle," the Deputy said. Another shot rang out.

"That's three, but they are too deep in the cover now," the Sheriff said. "I can't see any of them."

"Let's screw up their vehicles," Major Hobbs said. "Private, bring that mortar up here."

"Yes sir," said the private. He brought the mortar over and set it up, about thirty yards away from the trees that the blind was in.

{117}

"Alright, I'm going to guestimate the coordinates," Major Hobbs said. He talked quietly to the private, and made adjustments. "Good, let one go."

The private dropped a projectile into the mortar, and there was a roar, then a loud explosion.

"What was that?" the Sheriff asked.

"Mortar," Frank said.

"Excellent," the Sheriff said. "He was a little too far out. Have him bring it in about sixty yards."

Frank looked back at the Major.

"I heard him, Frank," he said. "You hear that private?"

"Yes sir," he said. He made the adjustment, and dropped another mortar round into the tube. There was an explosion, and then three other loud blasts."

"Yahooooo!" shouted the Sheriff. "You hit at least a couple of vehicles. Nice shooting."

"Alright, private, nice job," the Major said. "Keep hitting them. Vary it front, back, left, and right by about twenty yards. Let's screw that parking area up good."

"Yes sir," he said, and proceeded.

"Hey, Frank," the Sheriff said. "I see some guys running this way. Black outfits. Probably some of those Islamic pansies. I can get a couple, but we need a few guys down by the creek." He fired once, then fired again. "Two down, but that's all I can see."

"I'm going," Jerry said. "Time to try out this AK." He trotted over to the creek, and laid down behind a high spot on the bank.

A mortar round roared as Jerry got himself set.

Frank followed Jerry with Lucy. He got behind a tree next to the creek, and peered around. He couldn't see anybody. Then Lucy growled, and looked at a clump of bushes. Frank saw movement, and fired a shot with the Winchester. A fighter rolled out, holding his side, and Jerry hit him with three shots from the AK. Just then another

Bug Out! Part 3 – Motorhome Madness

fighter jumped up and started running towards Jerry. He yelled 'Allahu Akbar' as he charged, his gun in his hands.

"Oh, please," Jerry said, laughing, as he pulled the trigger, sending the fighter flying to the ground. "These guys are idiots, Frank."

Another mortar round fired off. There were more secondary explosions.

"Sounds like the Private hit pay dirt again," Jerry said, laughing.

"Watch your left flank, Jerry!" Frank yelled. He fired the Winchester at the running man, but missed. The fighter was running too fast. Then there was another blast…a big one, and the fighter flew to the ground.

"Take that, cretin," shouted Earl. He worked the bolt of his rifle to chamber another round.

"That's two I owe you now, Earl," Jerry shouted. Then he saw another out of the corner of his eye. He fired with the AK again, stopping him dead. Then there was silence.

Frank moved cautiously over to where Jerry was, Lucy by his side.

"Somebody has to go over to the parking area and clean things up."

"I'll take care of that, Frank," said a voice from behind him. It was Major Hobbs. He pulled out the field radio.

"Private, stop the mortar rounds now, we're going in."

"Will do, Major," the voice said over the scratchy sound of the radio.

"Alright, men, let's go in in groups of two. Fan out wide to catch any stragglers. If you can capture a couple of them, go for it, but don't put yourself at risk."

The soldiers spread and slowly moved forward, jumping over the creek and seeking some cover as soon as they got to the other side.

"What should we do?" Frank asked Jerry.

A few rifle shots came from the parking lot area.

"Sit tight for a few minutes," Jerry said.

Two rifle shots came the front of the park.

"They are trying to get into the front," Jerry said. "Those weren't military rounds. Those are big bore hunting rifles."

"Charlie and Jeb," Frank said. "They're on the roof of the store with their hunting rifles.

The sound of small arms fire from the front of the park filled the air.

"That's military," Jerry said. "I hope it's mostly our guys."

There were more large bore rifle shots. Then a mortar round went off, and there was a loud secondary explosion. Then more small arms fire, and more big bore rifle shots.

"Some heavy action going on up there – hope Jasmine and Rosie stay in the clubhouse….." Jerry said. Another mortar round stopped his conversation.

"Hey, guys," Captain Hobbs shouted from across the creek. "We're clear. You can come on back. Wait until you see what we found."

"Let's go," Jerry said. Frank nodded, and they both got up cautiously and headed for the parking area.

"Sounds like the action in the front has stopped," Frank said.

"Yeah, that could be good or bad."

"Wow, look at those trucks," Frank said. "Those are US Army vehicles."

The parking lot came fully into view. There were three army troop transport trucks. All were destroyed, and one of them still had a full load of soldiers when it was hit. There were mangled bodies of Islamist fighters all over the place.

"Look at that!" Jerry said, pointing.

"Is that what I think it is?" asked Frank as Major Hobbs was walking up.

"Sure is. That's a real live M-1 Battle Tank. The guys manning it must have had the hatch open and been outside. Everybody around it is dead."

Bug Out! Part 3 – Motorhome Madness

"Is the tank damaged?" asked Jerry.

"Naw, those small field mortars won't take out an M-1 unless they get a real lucky hit. I have my guys checking it out now."

"So how did these cretins get all of this US Army equipment?" asked Frank.

"These probably came from one of the bases that was overrun in New Mexico a few days ago," the Major said. "We're lucky that we hit that full transport truck with the mortar. There were another twelve men in the back. And they had two RPGs and a mortar, too."

"Any of it salvageable?" Frank asked.

"The mortar might be, but we don't have the time to mess with it," he said.

"We do," Jerry said, and he winked at Frank.

"Help yourself," Major Hobbs said. "Might have to clean it a little bit. It's a bloody mess."

"Anybody alive?" asked Frank.

"Nope," the Major said. "There were a few wounded men back there, but they tried to fire at us so we took them out. I'll bet we have a few who are trying to get away as we speak. Jerry, want to help us track them?"

"Hell, yes," Jerry said.

"Alright, go over there and help Private Bates. He's a good man, and knows some tracking as well."

"Alright, see you later, gentlemen."

Frank and Major Hobbs surveyed the scene as the privates slowly went through everything, stacking up weapons and ammo close to where the trail came over the creek.

"You've got more weapons," the Major said.

"You aren't taking them?"

"No, we've got plenty of small arms and ammo, and of course the ammo for these AKs isn't the same as ours. You guys should keep this stuff, and start moving away from the hunting rifles as soon you can."

{121}

"Oh, I don't know, this Winchester hasn't let me down yet," Frank said.

"I know, but it will. Those were never designed for the military. If you get some dirt in that action, it's going to jamb. It takes a while to reload those relics, too. Slipping a fresh magazine into an AK-47 is a lot better when you are in a fire fight."

"Yeah, probably a good point, I guess," Frank said.

"You guys have been extremely lucky in every one of these battles so far, Frank."

"I know."

"Good, because you need to prepare yourself. Some of you folks are going to get killed. It's only a matter of time."

"I understand that," Frank said. "If you guys weren't with us on this occasion, we'd probably still be in the heat of a very bad fight. That mortar helped a lot."

"They were going to get that tank's gun pointed at the park and start firing," the Major said. "That would have been it, and your small arms fire wouldn't have made a stitch of difference."

"We need to bottle up this area back here."

"Yes," the Major said. "I have some suggestions."

"Shoot," Frank said.

"After you get the bodies cleaned out of here, I'd use something to move the hulks of those trucks into the driveway over there. The trees around this place are going to make it really tough to get anything through if the driveway is blocked."

"Go on."

"Then back the tank up into this end of the parking lot, and point the gun right down the driveway. Have somebody man that sucker 24-7."

"You aren't taking the tank with you?"

"No, I can't use it," the Major said. "You guys just got yourself an expensive piece of hardware. I'll get you manuals as soon as I can, but we can probably have Lieutenant James check some of your folks out. He used to work with those."

"Have you been in contact with Major Darcy?"

"Not yet, trying to get him on the radio."

"Uh Oh, I hope everything is alright up there."

"If they lost, we'd still be hearing gunshots as the cretins execute all of the people in the park. Don't know if the battle is over yet, but we haven't lost."

"You noticed the big difference about this attack, didn't you, Major?" Frank asked.

"What?"

"No militia men."

The Major looked him in the eye, and had a worried expression.

{ 11 }

Dead Soldiers

The men stood in the forest behind the park, eyes darting around.

"You're right," Major Hobbs said. "I haven't seen any militia men anywhere back here. Only Islamist fighters. Even in the truck that we hit with the mortar round."

"Did you contact Major Darcy yet?" asked Frank.

"No, and that's worrisome," he said. "Feel like sneaking up there with me?"

"I was going either way. Jane is up there." Frank said.

"Alright, I'll let my privates know. You want to take anybody else?"

"I'd say Jerry, but he's tracking right now. Probably a good idea to keep him on that."

"OK," Major Hobbs said. He trotted over to where his men were going through the wreckage of the trucks, and let them know he would be gone for a few minutes. He rejoined Frank, and they walked towards the gate.

"Sheriff, we're going up front for a few minutes," Frank said as they went by the blind.

"Who?"

"Just Major Hobbs and I. If there aren't big problems, we'll be back in a few minutes."

"Alright, I'll keep an eye out. I'd leave that mortar there and sighted in on that parking lot just in case a second wave comes in here."

"Will do," Major Hobbs said. He went over to the private manning the mortar and told him to sit tight for now.

They walked through the gate. Everything looked normal, but nobody was walking around. It was like everybody took off and left the park empty.

"I'll sneak up to the clubhouse," Frank said.

"Alright, I'm going over by where the Humvees are parked."

Frank made his way to the clubhouse, and peered into one of the windows. Jane was sitting in there, next to Rosie and Jasmine and Chester. The doc was working on somebody up towards the front of the room with one of the paramedics, but he couldn't see who. He went around to the door. Jane saw him and ran over to him, hugging him tightly.

"Oh, Frank, I'm so glad you're okay." She kissed him and continued to hug him tightly. Jasmine came running over.

"Where's Jerry?" she said, tears streaming down her face.

"He's fine, don't worry. We won in the back. He's helping one of the privates back there track anybody who might have escaped."

"Thank God," she said. Rosie and Chester came hobbling over.

"Jerry alright?" Rosie asked.

"He's fine, mom," Jasmine said, smiling.

"Oh, crap, is that Hilda on the table?" Frank said.

"Yes, she got hit pretty badly," Jane said. "Doc said he thinks she will make it, but it's going to be touch and go for a little while."

"What happened up here?" Frank asked.

"It was horrible," Jane said. "The Islamist fighters came driving up the road towards us. Jeb and Charlie saw them, and took out the folks driving the front truck. They shot out the tires too. It bottled up the road, and the other trucks behind it couldn't get past it. It looked like we were going to take them all, when about half of Major Darcy's men turned. They shot him. Then they shot Hilda. The remaining good privates took them out."

"How is Major Darcy?" Frank asked.

"He's dead," Jane said.

"Oh, crap. Anybody else get hit?"

"No," Jane said.

"Jeb and Charlie saved our butts," Chester said. Those first shots at that truck were about 300 yards out. Took the cretins completely by surprise."

"Don't mess with rednecks," Frank said. The door opened, and Major Hobbs rushed in. He had tears on his face and a look of anger and resolve.

"We've only got six men left out there," Major Hobbs said. "I'm assuming you heard what happened to Major Darcy."

"Yes, Major. I'm so sorry," Frank said.

"Well, the only good news is that we know the remaining privates are real army. Between your two redneck friends and the roof of that store and what was left of Darcy's men, they were able to stop the enemy."

"How did they stop them out on the road?" Frank asked.

"Your friends took out that first truck, and it bottled up the street. Major Darcy was working with his gunner to get the mortar set up when he got shot by the plants. Then a battle went on between the remaining good privates and the bad guys. That was over pretty fast, but we lost another two good men."

"So after that, they got the mortar set up, I suspect."

"Yes, they did, and they blasted the two trucks that were behind the first one. They shot most of the Islamists as they jumped out and tried to run. A few of them got away, though. I've got four of the remaining privates chasing them down now. These 'fighters' were so flustered that they didn't even try to attack the campground. The Islamists talk a good game, but they ain't worth much against real men."

The Doc walked up.

"Hilda is going to make it, but she needs to be in bed for at least a few days," he said. "I got the bullet out, and the wound dressed. She lost a fair amount of blood, but the bullet didn't do any serious damage. She's a lucky gal."

"Thanks, Doc," Chester said.

"Does Charlie know?" Frank asked.

"Yes, he was down here with her until we started cutting to get the bullet out. Then he went back up to be with Jeb on the roof. I'll talk to him."

"Thanks, Doc," Frank said.

"You're going to have a problem getting out of here, at least for a while, I'm afraid," Major Hobbs said.

"Road pretty bottled up, eh?" he asked.

"Yes. When the privates get back from the chase, I'll get a couple of those Humvees out there to drag the wreckage out of the way. We'll also grab their supplies and bring them in here. More AK-47s and ammo to add to your arsenal. Maybe some grenades and mortars too."

"Yeah, those mortars come in handy," Frank said.

"We heard them going off back there. What happened?" Chester asked.

"The enemy brought three troop transport trucks and a tank into the back parking area," Frank said. We caught them flat footed with that mortar. Good thing, too, because they were getting the tank ready to start bombarding the park."

"Yeah, their strategy makes a lot of sense, actually," Major Hobbs said. "Attack from the rear, and have forces up front to stop us from escaping. We were very lucky."

"How did you take the tank out?" asked Jane.

"We didn't take out the tank, but the men manning the tank were outside when the mortar fire hit them. That tank is in working order."

"Really?" asked Chester. "What kind?"

"M-1 Battle tank," Major Hobbs said. "I think you guys should man that thing back there in addition to watching from the blind."

"I know quite a bit about tanks," Chester said. "Learned about them in the service. Nothing newer than M-60s, but I've kept up. Maybe I can help."

"Maybe," Major Hobbs said. "That reminds me, how is Lieutenant James doing, Doc?"

"He's less injured than I thought. I was going to release him this afternoon, but got the call to come down here. If you can get me back into town, I'll get him released and you can bring him back here."

"Excellent," Major Hobbs said. "He's an expert on the M-1 tanks. He can help get a bunch of your folks checked out on that thing."

"I did have one thought since we talked, Major," Frank said. "I'm not so sure that it's a good idea to bottle up that back parking area in such a way that we can't get out there."

"Why? No way could you get any motor homes through to that parking lot."

"I know, but we could fix things so that we could get cars through there. Most of us have TOADs"

"What's a TOAD?" asked the Major.

"It's a vehicle that you tow behind your motor home," Chester said.

"Oh. Well, you may have a point there, Frank. I'll leave that one up to you. If you are smart with that tank and have it manned all the time, nobody is getting through there."

{129}

One of the privates rushed in.

"Major Hobbs, our men are back," he said."

"Thanks, private," the Major said. "Send them in."

The four men came in.

"Well, anything?" he asked.

"There were three of them walking away. We killed all of them, sir," said one of the privates.

"Private Finch, correct?"

"Yes sir," he replied.

"Any evidence of other vehicles that might have gotten away?"

"No sir, I'm almost sure of that," he said.

"How?"

"They would have had to make a K-turn to get out of there, and there were no tire tracks on the sides of the road or the turnout there," he said. "No way could they have pulled off a K-turn on the asphalt."

"Good job, Private Finch. Now we have another job to do. Let's get a couple Humvees out there and pull those busted trucks out of the road."

"Yes, sir," Private Finch said.

"Oh, and collect all of the weapons and ammo and bring them in here. Same for any grenades, mortars, or RPGs."

"Will do, sir," he said, and the four men turned and left.

Charlie walked in, and came up to the doc.

"How's my girl?" he asked.

"She's still doing well, but she needs bed rest for a few days," the doc said. "Anybody here know anything about nursing? The dressings will need to be changed."

"I nurse," Rosie said. "In Philippines."

"Good," the doc said. "Let's go over there and talk, and I'll show you what you need to do."

"OK," she said, and they walked over. "You have girlfriend?" The doc looked at her and laughed.

"Mom!" Jasmine said. Everybody else cracked up.

"What's the plan, guys?" asked Charlie.

"You missed out on that conversation we had earlier," Frank said. "When you guys were scouting the back for the cameras. Major Darcy and Major Hobbs told us what the situation is."

"Go on," Charlie said.

"The army has two problems right now. They are heavily tied up fighting inside Mexico, to stop the flow of Islamists and radicals from South America, and to re-take that country. It's going well, but it's left us thin up here. That's problem number one."

"What's problem number two?"

"You saw it today. The army has been infiltrated with a lot of recent immigrants who aren't really immigrants. They are plants from the South American radical groups. They've been doing just what we saw happen here today. They are very difficult to detect."

"That's not good."

"There are actually three problems," Major Hobbs said as he walked back over to them. "The other big problem is a very large movement of Islamist forces over the border from Canada."

"Yeah, I was getting to that," Frank said.

"So we are being attacked from the great white north and there is not enough army to handle them."

"Exactly. You know what that means?"

"Yes," Charlie said. "It means the citizens are in this fight too."

"Exactly," Frank said. Major Hobbs nodded in agreement.

"So we need to do more than just defend this place and try to stay alive," Charlie said. "We've got to take it to the enemy."

"Yes, that is the situation we are in now, I'm afraid," Major Hobbs said. "From what I've seen of you guys, you are up to the challenge. But let's be realistic. Some of you are going to get killed."

"Yes, that is what I'm afraid of," Jane said.

"Me too," Jasmine said.

"You two grow up," Rosie said, hobbling over. "You live here in US of A and never have to fight for freedom. You don't know what like to live in other places. You support your men. You fight. America worth this." She stared at the two of them as if they were both their daughters.

"Rosie is right," Major Hobbs said. "We could lose this country. Lord knows some of our leadership has done their best to make that happen, just by being lazy, stupid, and corrupt."

Suddenly they heard a metallic screeching sound out front. Everybody except Major Hobbs looked concerned.

"They are towing those trucks out of the roadway," the Major said. "I'd better go out and take a look at how they are doing."

"I'll go with you," Frank said.

"I'm going back on the roof to keep watch with Jeb, just in case," Charlie said. He headed for the store.

"Where are you dragging those hulks? In the front parking lot?" Frank asked.

"No, we don't need anything out there for bad guys to hide behind. We're going to put them in the turnouts along the bend of the road. That will make it hard for those guys to escape, should they come down that road again."

There was a pile of AK-47s, grenades, ammo, and three mortars with boxes of shells sitting next to the gate.

"Nice haul," Major Hobbs said. "Before we leave I'll make sure several of your folks know how to operate those mortars."

"Wonder if we'll get hit again today?" asked Frank.

"I doubt it, but this isn't over."

Frank's cell phone rang. The two men looked at each other and smiled. Frank pulled it out of his pocket and saw it was the Sheriff.

"Frank?"

"Sheriff, how's it going back there?"

"No more problems. The cell towers are back up. They just called me a few minutes ago and let me know."

"Wow that was quick."

"Just cut wires, apparently. They didn't bust up the tower or anything like that."

"How are you and the Deputy holding up there?"

"Fine. I think the army is wrapping things up down below. They got the tank moved to the back of the parking area, pointing outward. If anybody tries coming down that driveway, they won't have a good day."

"Good. Did they block off the driveway with those trucks yet?"

"No, Jerry told them to hold up on that. He thinks we should have an escape route out of here."

"Great minds think alike," Frank said. "I was going to suggest that too."

"They tracked one guy.....it was a wounded fighter that had tried to walk away. He bled out.....was dead before Jerry and the private found him. Doesn't sound like anybody else escaped."

"Good. We were damn lucky," Frank said. "We weren't so lucky up here."

"What happened?"

"The other Major got killed, by plants in his own force. It happened right as some bad guys were trying to get more troop transport trucks up to the front of the park. It was a coordinated effort."

"Sorry to hear that. I'll bet Charlie and Jeb stopped those trucks."

"Good guess. We got a good haul of supplies. More AK-47s and ammo, some mortars, and some other stuff."

"Good. I'm going to get off now, need to make some more calls into town. I'll get back to you."

"Alright, thanks, Sheriff."

Frank hung up the phone and put it in his pocket.

"Who fixed the cell tower?" asked Major Hobbs.

"Somebody in town. Apparently all the bad guys did was cut a few wires. They didn't knock the whole tower down."

"Good. Wonder if there is anybody in town that could guard it?"

"Don't know. I'll mention that to the Sheriff the next time I talk to him. He might already be on that. He said he had to call some people in town."

"How big is that town, anyway?"

"You know, I have no idea," Frank said. "I haven't been there myself yet. The Doc would know. Why?"

"I'm just wondering why they would bother messing with an RV park when there is a nice town nearby, that's all."

"Well, I used to think it was because of spooky dude," Frank said.

"Who's spooky dude?"

"Officer Simmons," Frank said. "I don't know what to think now, though. It doesn't appear that the militia and the Islamists are still working together."

"Oh, yeah, I remember now. You shot that guy on the way out of Williams."

"What do you know about him?" Frank asked.

"Not much more than rumors. That idiot Franklin P. whatever said that he was the main reason he lost control of the Williams militia, but I don't trust what that guy says."

There was more metallic screeching, and the last of the trucks was now out of the road. The privates got into the Humvees and drove back through the gate.

"All done, sir," one of the Privates said as he walked up.

"Good. Could you guys move the booty into the clubhouse, please? Stack it on one of the tables, and then find out who knows the most about how the mortars operate. We'll need to train some of these civilians on them."

Bug Out! Part 3 – Motorhome Madness

"Yes sir," he said, and he turned and walked over to the other privates. They got to work hauling things into the clubhouse."

"How much longer are you guys going to stick around?" Frank asked. They were walking back towards the clubhouse.

"I don't know. I'll have to get in touch with the CO and tell him what happened here. That's next on my list of things to do. It's not going to be fun. Darcy and the CO went way back."

One of the privates came running up.

"Major, somebody is trying to get you on the radio," he said.

"Thanks, private." He ran over to his Humvee and answered.

Frank continued on to the clubhouse, but the Major caught him at the door.

"That was the CO. He said a CIA guy is coming over right now to talk with us. He ought to be here any minute."

"Alright, maybe he's got some helpful info," Frank said.

"Hell, those folks don't give info, they take info," the Major said. He laughed. They both heard a car coming. It was an Arizona State Police car. It drove through the gate and over to where they were standing.

"Major Hobbs?"

"Yes," he said.

"Your CO just called you about me, correct?"

"Yes, CIA, right?"

"Yes. We need to talk." He got out of the car, and Frank finally got a good look at his face. It was Officer Simmons.

To be continued in Bug Out Part 4!

ABOUT THE AUTHOR

Robert G Boren is a writer from the South Bay section of Southern California. He writes Short Stories, Novels, and Serialized Fiction.